RECKLESS SURRENDER

THE SURRENDER SERIES, BOOK THREE

ZOE BLAKE

Poison Ink Publications

Copyright © 2018, 2021 by Zoe Blake & Poison Ink Publications

All rights reserved.
No part of this book may be reproduced in any form or by any electronic or mechanical means, including information storage and retrieval systems, without written permission from the author, except for the use of brief quotations in a book review.
Cover Design by Dark City Designs:

CONTENTS

Chapter 1	1
Chapter 2	6
Chapter 3	19
Chapter 4	31
Chapter 5	50
Chapter 6	59
Chapter 7	64
Chapter 8	77
Chapter 9	91
Chapter 10	96
Chapter 11	107
Chapter 12	120
Chapter 13	127
Chapter 14	138
Chapter 15	149
Epilogue	155
About Zoe Blake	159
Also by Zoe Blake	161

CHAPTER 1

Hush now, Phoebe, do not you fear
Never mind, Phoebe, the Mad Monk is near

THE SICKLY SWEET sing-song voice echoed around her empty bedchamber. Phoebe's mouth opened, the lower lip trembling in a macabre pantomime of a silent scream. Fear kept her immobile. A fear so intense it struck straight through her, making her very bones feel brittle and weak. A cold sweat broke out over her brow as she searched the darkness in vain, trying to peer past the moving shadows. Every outline was suspect. Every hint of sound, real or imagined, a cry of alarm, but there was nothing. Through the distorted glass of her window, she could see the burnt orange and crimson glow from the macabre dance of flickering flames as black-cloaked figures ran about with torches, the earlier torrential rain doing nothing to dampen the morbid celebration.

Casting a glance to her left, she could see a faint halo

of light surrounding the cracks at the edges of the door. Through it was the dark outline of a heavy bolt. The door was locked tight. Of course, someone had managed to get into her locked room before this.

It had been a warning.

A warning to stay away, to leave this place.

A warning she was putting herself in danger.

A warning she had ignored.

It was a small, single-room chamber with just enough space for a bed, desk and cozy chair in the corner. Barely larger than a student's dorm room. Surely she would know if someone had entered the chamber.

Leaning over, she flicked the switch to the dome ceiling light. Phoebe both craved the security the brightness would bring and dreaded what it might show.

Nothing happened.

Darkness still reigned.

She felt a fresh wave of terror. It took Phoebe a moment to recall she had removed the light bulb herself earlier in case *he* had tried to search her room looking for her. She'd wanted the darkness to shield her, to hide her from his prying, intense gaze, but now she wondered what else the darkness was hiding. Had someone else learned of her true purpose for being there? Learned about the lies she'd told to get to the truth?

Again, she scanned the darkness. The chamber was silent and still save for the distant shouts and cries from those outside.

Maybe she was just imagining it?

Her nerves were already strung tight from hiding from *him*…from *lying* to him. It only made sense her imagination would lean toward the dark and forboding, that her mind would conjure up monsters under the bed and a mad monk specter to go bump in the night.

Hush now, Phoebe, do not you fear
Never mind, Phoebe, the Mad Monk is near

The raspy voice was definitely coming from inside her bedchamber.

Phoebe launched herself at the door. Throwing the bolt, she ran into the hallway. She was halfway down the long corridor before the chill of the flagstone seeped through her thin socks. In her haste, she had not even grabbed her boots. Throwing a nervous look over her shoulder, she saw the corridor remained empty. The darkness was broken by shafts of weak, bloodstained light. Its source a row of tall, cathedral windows along one wall. Each window had a ruby red cross of Saint John in its center, a remnant from the school's monastic past. A luminous full moon shown through each cross, bathing the space in an eerie red glow.

Keeping an eye on the empty corridor, Phoebe reached into her back pocket for her phone. Needing a sense of safety no matter how meager, she leaned against the cold stone wall, protecting her back. She pressed the power button and waited for the screen to come to life.

No bars.

The earlier storm must have knocked out what passed for cell service in this remote area. Phoebe didn't even know who she would call. The police? Would they even dare to cross through the gates onto the property? Probably not. Worse, they would probably just call *him* and expect him to handle the situation. At that very moment, she wasn't certain what she was more afraid of…the possible murderer haunting her…or *his* wrath when he found out she had disobeyed him.

One thing was for certain, she needed to keep moving. Needed to find someplace to hide. Someplace no one would think to look for her.

For a brief moment, she wondered if she dared to return to her chamber for her boots, but then thought better of it. She would go to the gymnasium. The locker room would be a bright open space and perhaps she could borrow a pair of shoes from one of the open lockers.

With at least an immediate plan in place, Phoebe headed off down the corridor, feeling more confident the further away she got from the twisted rhyme and whoever was singing it. Stopping before a somber-looking portrait of some old man in a white wig who seemed to be staring down at her in disapproval, Phoebe tried to remember where the gym was in the labyrinth of old hallways and buildings.

The moment's distraction cost her dearly.

A strong arm wrapped around her middle as a large hand covered her mouth, stifling any hope of a scream for help. The hard, unrelenting form pressed along her back radiated masculine strength. Phoebe kicked out as her nails clawed at the hand covering her lips. Desperate to escape, she tried twisting and turning her body. The band of muscle wrapped tightly across her stomach squeezed harder, pressing painfully into her ribs, cutting off her air. Wrenching her head to one side, Phoebe tried to break his grasp. Her stockinged toes scraped along the flagstone for purchase as, with his superior strength, he easily lifted her off her feet.

Still, she fought.

Then she heard a deep, throaty chuckle.

Warm lips skimmed the shell of her left ear. She could feel the faint touch of his breath along the exposed delicate skin of her neck. Inhaling precious air through her nose, she caught the spicy scent of his cologne.

"I warned you what would happen if you defied me, princess."

Phoebe's bright green eyes grew wide at the darkly whispered threat cloaked in an endearment. Her pleas were muffled nonsense from beneath his hand.

Already lightheaded from her fevered gasps for breath, she failed to fight when he shifted his grasp to effortlessly lift her over one powerful shoulder.

"You need to learn that no one…no one…defies my command."

She could feel him pivot. Just as he crossed a threshold and slammed the door shut behind them, she reclaimed her voice.

The faint echo of her cry was swallowed by the dark shadows of the cold, uncaring stone corridor.

CHAPTER 2

Two weeks earlier.

PHOEBE GRIMACED as the deafening screech of an out of tune saxophone blared in her ear. Casting a glare over her shoulder at the street performer dressed as Spiderman playing a disgraceful version of *Amazing Grace*, she stepped off the curb...straight into a pothole. The unexpected jolt caused her ankle to twist as she spilled her mocha latte down the front of her black and purple pinstriped suit.

"Damn it," cursed Phoebe as the right heel snapped off her black pump. As she bent down to retrieve the heel, a taxi horn blared angrily. "All right! All right! I'm moving!" she shouted in the direction of the New York yellow cab before hobbling across the crosswalk. Tossing the heel in her shoulder bag, she vainly rummaged around for a napkin or tissue to wipe off her suit. "Too bad people don't carry handkerchiefs anymore," she muttered under her breath as she swiped at the droplets of creamy chocolate liquid clinging to the fabric of her skirt. Tossing the now-empty coffee cup in the trash, she made her way down the block to the offices of the *New York Ledger*.

Emerging from the glass revolving door into the large, marble floored lobby, she tilted up her chin in greeting to the security guard. "Hey, Matt."

"Morning, Phoebe," replied Matt without looking up from the racing form he was studying. "They're waiting for you in Henry's office."

"I know." She pressed the button for the elevator as she took another rueful swipe at her still-damp skirt. *At least it had missed her silk blouse*, she thought with a pained smile.

Hobbling out of the elevator on the fifteenth floor, Phoebe gave the receptionist a quick wave as she walked past to her cubicle.

The receptionist covered the mouthpiece of her headphones and leaned over her desk to call out, "Henry's waiting for you in his office."

"I know," responded Phoebe over her shoulder without turning around.

Limping to her desk, she sat down with a huff. Unbuckling both ankle straps, she pulled off her black pumps. Opening the bottom drawer of her desk, she surveyed the random selection of shoes: a pair of black high heels and a red pair of flats, some old worn sneakers and a pair of slippers. Selecting the black high heels, she was placing them on her feet when a bespectacled face appeared over the gray wall of her cubicle.

"What are you doing? Henry's waiting."

Jimmy was the assistant to the assistant editor at the *Ledger*. Basically, an all-around jimmy-on-the-spot, go-to man for the staff. Unfortunately, he looked like an even nerdier version of Leonard from *The Big Bang Theory*, complete with glasses and a rather eclectic collection of comic book T-shirts. He also looked to be about sixteen despite his age of thirty-two. Of course, the comic book T-shirts didn't help.

"So I've heard," quipped Phoebe as she rose out of her seat, grabbed her spiral notebook and followed Jimmy into Henry Cobb's office.

"Helluva job, Wilson. Helluva job!" exclaimed Henry, the Chief Editor of the *Ledger*, as he lifted his considerable bulk out of his long-suffering office chair to greet her.

In the five years since she had been at the *Ledger* working her way up from intern to investigative journalist, Henry had never, not once, called her by her first name, Phoebe. She was always 'Wilson' to him. Phoebe figured it was his way of coping with the regrettable fact…at least to him…that she was a female. Despite his old boys' club tendencies, Henry was an amazing boss and the closest thing she had to a father.

Laughing, Phoebe plucked the cigar from his fingers and snubbed it out in the ashtray, which was a permanent fixture on the right-hand corner of his desk.

"You don't ever snub out a cigar," he complained. "That's sacrilege."

Giving him an admonishing look, she said, "You promised no cigars before noon. You can at least wait till then before you completely ignore all your doctor's orders for the day."

Mumbling something about meddling females, Henry lowered himself into his chair behind his desk. Tapping one pudgy finger on the folded newspaper there, he repeated, "Helluva job! I hear the FBI is now getting involved."

"It will take me another week to get the stench of fryer oil out of my hair but it was worth it." Phoebe smiled with pride as she took a seat across from him.

She had spent the last month undercover as a hostess in Chinatown. It had taken forever to just get the job and even longer to sneak into the owner's office to grab peeks at his financial records. Being suspicious of computers, Lee Woo had kept everything on paper, which had actually helped her investigation. Hacking into someone's computer was a pain in the ass; she much preferred paper files. It was because of Woo's anxiety over the government spying on his computer that she had been able to get copies of all the documentation she'd needed to prove he was cheating his employees. Paying them far less than minimum wage, and sometimes not paying them at all. Forcing the cooks in the kitchen to work long hours and failing to compensate them for overtime. Cheating the IRS by underreporting the revenue he brought in at his twelve, cash-only, restaurants throughout Chinatown. It was her article that had brought down the 'King of Chinatown' and led to the FBI raiding his offices earlier this morning.

"*Associated Press* has picked up the article. Should hit wide by tomorrow," said Henry as he shuffled a large pile of papers from one side of the desk to the other.

"That's great exposure for the *Ledger*," observed Phoebe.

Henry smirked. "Even better for you. One of these days the *Post* or *Times* are going to steal you away from me."

Phoebe looked about the office with its cheap mismatched furniture and faded artwork. "And leave all this luxury?" she joked, giving Henry a playful wink.

Henry snapped his fingers at Jimmy who had been standing patiently by his desk. Jimmy quickly handed him one of the files he was holding.

"I know you are working on that crooked cop from—"

"Florida. I was, but the trail went cold fast. We know he escaped from that prison in Florida and allegedly stole a car and is going after some ex-girlfriend. All I've really got so far is a bunch of conflicting witnesses stating they've seen him in their neighborhood. I guess I'll have to go interview—"

"No, nix that. Everybody and their dog is chasing that story. Let them waste time and money running around all over the place in what will most likely be a wild goose chase. I've got a real story for you. An exclusive lead. This one comes straight from the top."

Intrigued, Phoebe raised one eyebrow. "Is it juicy?" she asked, leaning forward to try to catch a glimpse of the folder in his hand, all the while smiling because she knew Henry hated the word juicy.

Giving her a grimace, he said, "Well, you don't get any *juicier* than murder."

Phoebe fell back into her chair with a disappointed

huff. "I don't do murder. Obituaries are Sam's department."

"Come on, Wilson. You know the old adage, if it bleeds it leads. Besides, this came straight from the top."

"The owner? How is he possibly involved in a murder? Did an old fraternity brother stab his trophy wife with a sharpened oyster spoon?"

Henry tossed the folder on his desk toward her. "Two women were ritualistically murdered. Strangled and some weird satanic symbol was carved into their chests. One was the daughter of a close friend of the paper. He wants this story out and the murderer found, thinks some press on the issue would help."

Phoebe opened the folder and looked over the memo from Grant Richards, the owner of the *New York Ledger*, as Henry continued to talk. Then, glimpsing some skin with dark brown dried blood, she snapped the file shut. The photos were a bit much to look at before her latte had kicked in.

"Whole matter is being hushed up. Police were barely even involved in the investigation. Rubber-stamped the military's conclusions."

Phoebe looked up. "The owner asked for me specifically." She had wanted to sound nonchalant but there was no keeping the awe and excitement out of her voice.

"Welcome to the big leagues, kid." Henry reached for another cigar and held a match in front of the rolled tobacco, heating it.

Phoebe watched the tip glow a bright, angry red as she quickly surmised what this could mean for her career. She had no desire to be a little fish in the big swirling vortex of the pond of those larger New York newspapers, but she so very much wanted to be a big fish in the *Ledger* pond.

Focusing on the matter at hand, she asked, "Why are the police not involved in the main investigation?"

"It happened on the grounds of the Puller Military Academy where one of the teachers was a victim. It's a distinguished naval school with a lot of powerful alumni. Local cops didn't stand a chance. They're blaming some mysterious homeless man, the *go-to* story when no one wants to find the real killer. My money is on some senator's son the military is protecting."

Phoebe nodded as she took in the information. It was a fairly straightforward story. Influential, probably extremely competitive school would do anything to not have a salacious murder attached to their name. It also didn't surprise her that the Navy would want to handle the matter internally.

"We're moving fast on this one," said Henry, interrupting her thoughts. "Jimmy, show her what you got."

Eager to show off what he had accomplished, Jimmy straightened his glasses and rummaged through the remaining files in his arms. "Building off your own credentials of a Master's in English Literature, we created a new identity for you and got you a position as an assistant professor of English at the academy."

Her eyebrow quirked up as Phoebe huffed in disbelief. "I'm assuming this is a prestigious school, and they just hired me without an interview?"

"They're desperate. You'll be replacing the teacher who was just murdered. Not many clamoring for the position," Henry interjected.

"Lucky me," joked Phoebe.

"Some of the other teachers are spooked and have left mid-term. They need bodies. No pun intended. Plus Mr. Richards greased a few wheels with the board to get you past all the usual hiring nonsense. You start in two days," continued Henry.

"Two days! That barely gives me time to pack let alone do background research!"

"You can research while you're there. They need you there as soon as possible. The term has already started."

Jimmy handed Phoebe the file with her fake credentials and identification. Phoebe opened the file and immediately shot to her feet.

"What the fuck, Jimmy? Eustace Pringle? Seriously?" she asked incredulously.

Holding his hands up defensively, Jimmy rushed to explain. "We needed you to sound older so they wouldn't question the hire. My grandmother's name is Eustace so I figured that would work."

"The idea is that once you are there, they won't turn you away when they learn you're barely twenty-one—" explained Henry.

"Twenty-six," interrupted Phoebe.

"Whatever. The point is no one is knocking down their doors to grab the open teaching positions, so you'll be in."

Casting them both a disgruntled glare, Phoebe looked over the travel itinerary. "Buzzards Bay! You are sending me to a place called Buzzards Bay?"

Rising, Henry patted her on the shoulder as he

ushered her out of his office. "Think of it as a vacation. I know you secretly hate the city."

"Buzzards Bay is not a vacation, Henry. It sounds like a place where pirates hide dead bodies."

"There you go! You already have the opening line to your murder article. See? You are perfect for this story."

Phoebe turned to toss a harsh rejoinder over her shoulder, but Henry's door was already closed.

Jimmy stood sheepishly by her side. "I got you a ticket with as few connecting flights as possible," he offered as a feeble mea culpa.

"First class?" she asked hopefully.

"Yeah, right," he snorted.

Phoebe turned to stomp off.

"Have fun in Buzzards Bay, Professor Pringle," he shouted after her retreating back, laughing as she raised a middle finger in response.

* * *

PHOEBE LOOKED over the rims of her black, cat-eye sunglasses. They were really just for show. The weather beyond the taxi window was wet and dull. Grim would be a better word. The rundown Camry proclaiming itself a 'taxi' in Sharpie on a plain piece of white paper on the dash was the best she could find after landing at the local airport. It wound through countless country lanes before breaking out onto a two-lane highway that followed the coast. She watched as foamy sprays of water splashed up on the jagged rocks. Looking out over the Atlantic, the ocean appeared gray and bleak. In the far distance, there was a lighthouse. Usually cheery beacons for travelers, this one had an ominous appearance. As if a large black spider were floating above the salt spray.

"That's the entrance light to Buzzards Bay," the driver helpfully offered.

"It's…ah…pretty," Phoebe politely responded.

They continued to circle round the bay.

"It's a bit foggy today but to the left…that's Puller Military Academy," said the driver.

Phoebe eagerly slid to the other side of the back seat to get a glimpse. At first, all she could see were a pair of turrets peeking out above the dark trees. Then a clearing opened up. Her teeth bit into her lower lip, a nervous tic to hide her trepidation. The misty fog and weak sun prevented a crisp view, but she could just make out the harsh angles of the imposing structure. It looked like a medieval castle rising high above the land. Somber and authoritative. Built of gray stone, it was at least eight stories high with two turrets that stretched even higher. The dark windows gave a hint of possible stained glass images. All that was missing was a drawbridge. It was surrounded by numerous lower buildings all built of the same drab stone. Phoebe would have expected that a military academy's landscaping would be neat and structured, rigid almost, but that was not the case here. The surrounding area looked almost wild. It was a large tapestry of bright and dark colors from the green pitch pines, scrub oaks and ferns to the red maples and blueberry bushes which grew unheeded throughout the grounds. It all led to a high cliff that overlooked the deep, churning bay.

"It's actually an old monastery. Navy took it over sometime in the early 1920s. Been an academy ever since." The driver chatted cheerily on as they rounded a curve and all that was left was a view of the academy flag, a brief flash of color as it flew proudly above one of the turrets.

The rest of the drive continued in silence.

As much as she had an obligation to stay objective, Phoebe had to admit it certainly *looked* like the type of place where murderers lurked in the dark shadows.

* * *

THE TAXI DROVE OFF, lightly kicking up dust and stones from the white gravel driveway.

Any hope Phoebe had had that Herring Run was actually a quaint Massachusetts bed and breakfast was dashed. It was actually the Herring Run Motel. Funny how Jimmy had left the motel part off the travel itinerary. When she got back, she was going to kick him in the shins or maybe tell him Ben Affleck was the best Batman there ever was. Either option would hurt him.

At least it looked cute and clean, thought Phoebe as she surveyed the gray walls, black shingles and red doors. Although, what was with this area and the color gray?

The small bell over the door gave off a bright jingle as she entered the motel office.

She greeted the older gentleman behind the counter with a smile. "Hello, my name is…Eustace Pringle. I believe my office made a reservation."

"We have you right here. Don't get many visitors up this way in October. Will that be a credit card?"

"No. I'll be paying in cash. Just the one night."

"Visiting family?"

"No, I'm a new assistant professor at the military academy," offered Phoebe. She might as well start working on her cover now and besides, it would be good to possibly get a local's perspective on the school.

The man gave a low whistle and looked at her with concern. "It's none of my business, but you seem like a sweet girl. I would hop right back in a taxi and get back to where you came from if I were you."

"Why do you say that?"

The man gave a conspiratorial look to his left then to his right, despite their being the only two people in the tiny, cramped office, before leaning over the counter and beckoning her closer. "The place is haunted by the damned," he whispered.

"My, my…haunted?" Phoebe played along with bemusement.

"By the mad monk. Back in 1666, two monks came to the area to convert the local Indians to Christianity. Story goes they got lost in the forest. Weeks later when they were found, one of the monks had gone mad. Eaten the other one. The mad monk turned into what the Indians call a wendigo, an evil spirit, who haunts the woods to this day."

A mad cannibalistic monk. A haunted castle…or at least castle-like building. Her story was shaping up, thought Phoebe with a hidden smile.

Phoebe leaned in closer. "Do you think that's what happened to those two poor women?"

"Heard about that did you?"

Phoebe nodded her head.

Again the man took a cautious look to his left then right.

"I wouldn't be surprised. There is evil in those woods. More deaths are coming, mark my words."

On that happy, crazy, superstitious note, Phoebe got her room key and went back out into the salty air. Rolling her large suitcase down the narrow sidewalk, she stopped at the crimson door with the gold metal plate displaying the number three. Letting herself in and abandoning her suitcase at the door, she immediately grabbed her shoulder bag and pulled out the color-coded files and her laptop. Placing all the tourist brochures and to-go menus to the side to make a clean working space, she laid out her materials, grabbed her notebook and started to scribble down some initial impressions.

Firing up her computer, she intended to research the history of Puller Military Academy but gave in to the temptation to see what she could find online about the mad monk.

CHAPTER 3

*L*ieutenant Colonel Michael Lawson entered his new office. Compared to a tent in Fallujah, it was exceedingly luxurious. A large, polished oak desk dominated the space. The walls were covered in a deep navy blue wallpaper with gold embossed anchors. The bookshelves were filled with old books that no one had cracked a spine on in probably over five decades. His polished boots sunk into the thick Persian carpet that covered much of the heavily varnished hardwood floor. He hated that. He liked to hear the sound of his own footsteps and those of anyone approaching. He would have talked to his secretary, Mrs. Ludtz, about having it removed if he hadn't feared it would give the poor woman apoplexy. It was readily apparent this academy was her whole world. A world that should not be tampered with in any way, shape or form in her opinion. In short, she was a traditionalist. Despite her polite demeanor, he was fairly certain she'd hated him on the spot.

For starters, he was a Marine.

Puller Military Academy was a naval college, and although the Marines pulled from the Reserve Officer Training Corps body of midshipmen upon graduation same as the Navy, the school was primarily viewed as a naval institution. As such, the superintendent of the school, traditionally, had always been an admiral in the Navy.

In addition to not being an admiral in the Navy, at only thirty-six Michael was also one of the youngest Lieutenant Colonels in the Marine Corps. Instead of a distinguished and more-appropriate-for-the-academy…sixty-five…in Mrs. Ludtz's oft-shared opinion.

The final nail in his coffin where the secretary was concerned was that Michael had been brought in specifically to put the school on lockdown since the murders. The Navy had stonewalled the local cops from investigating too deeply but that hadn't meant they didn't want answers. If there was a murderer among their ranks, they wanted him found…quickly and quietly…before there were any more deaths. Michael's previous experiences abroad made him especially suited to the task.

Michael assumed her objections were to even the slightest implication that a distinguished member of the academy would be involved in something as low-brow as murder. His presence underscored that the Navy thought it was a possibility and that probably rankled her.

So in addition to his age, rank, branch of service and stated purpose already being black marks against him, Michael feared the removal of the rug would probably do the poor woman in.

Captain Mark Dobson rose from his chair in front of

the desk the moment he saw Michael. Captain Dobson was his Commandant of Midshipmen. The equivalent of a dean of students at a regular civilian school. A smart, capable man...who also bitterly resented Michael's new appointment to superintendent almost as much as Mrs. Ludtz, although he went to a great deal more effort to hide it than she did.

"Good afternoon, Mark," greeted Michael as he waved the man back into his chair and took his own seat behind the desk. "I've been reviewing your report on the security measures at the school."

"Yes, Commander. As you can see, I have a very qualified midshipman first class in charge of regular patrols."

"Yes. Excellent, but more needs to be done. I want surprise bunk checks each week. I also want to see the files on any midshipman who may seem troubled since arriving at the academy."

Mark fidgeted in his chair. "I'm not sure what you are referring to, sir."

Michael gave Mark an assessing look. Slowly lowering the report he was reviewing, he turned his intense dark gaze on the man, all hint of convivial conversation gone. "I want the files of any man you think capable of strangling a woman with his bare hands and then carving up her body, is that clearer for you, Captain?"

The academy had a stringent application process and accepted fewer than three percent of applicants but that didn't mean a bad apple did not occasionally slip through. In fact, in his experience, the type of sociopath capable of this kind of murder was probably highly efficient and intelligent, something that would look good to the academy.

Mark lowered his gaze. "Yes, sir," he responded quietly. "There was no evidence it was a midshipman…sir. You won't make any friends on campus by treating them all as suspects."

"I'm not here to make friends," countered Michael with a frown as he tossed the report aside. "And I would thank you not to prevaricate in the future when I ask you a direct question. You are dismissed."

"Yes, sir. I will get you those files."

Mark rose and departed, quietly. *Damn that fucking rug.* You could read a lot about a man's inner thoughts by the measure and sound of his gait as he walked toward or away from you.

Although Michael didn't need any additional clues to know what Mark was thinking.

Michael had been appointed superintendent to oversee a complete overhaul of the school's security and find a killer. It was the opinion of the upper brass and the board that regulations had become lax under the previous superintendent. Standards lowered. Even if the murderer wasn't a staff member or part of the student body, the murders themselves should never have been able to take place unnoticed on military property. It was an embarrassment.

They wanted fresh eyes and a fresh perspective on the place. Someone with authority and the energy to see the job done. After four tours oversees, Michael was more than ready for a domestic challenge. Besides his stated purpose, he liked the idea of helping shape the future of both the Navy and the Marines.

His only worry was what would happen once the task of finding the murderer and getting the school back on track was complete. Could he settle down into the quiet routine of the academy? Would he find it too boring and mundane to keep his interest? It was going to be difficult to compete with the constant excitement of being on tour, thought Michael.

There was something not quite right about this school, something almost dangerous. He would find out what it was and tackle the problem the only way a Marine knew how—head-on.

"Commander, the new assistant professor is here to meet you."

Mrs. Ludtz broke into his thoughts as she entered his office unannounced and without permission.

There was a disgusted tone to her voice that should have caught his attention but didn't.

"Send them in," he responded without looking up from his keyboard.

The office was silent save for the clicking and clacking of the keys as he rapidly typed his response to several outstanding emails.

Someone cleared their throat.

Michael lifted startled eyes to take in the woman standing before him. He had not heard her approach. *Damn that rug.* A man needed a warning before a woman like this approached him, if only to watch the sway of her hips as she did.

God damn, she was gorgeous.

Sleek, shiny blonde hair fell in waves past her shoulders. Creamy pale skin set off full lips covered in a bright, fuck-me, red lipstick. She wore a light purple silk blouse. He could just make out the rippled impression of what was surely a lace bra snugly holding ample breasts. A straight black skirt that ended in some sort of ruffle just above her knees emphasized the swell of her hips. He couldn't believe he was thinking this but even her ankles looked sexy as hell as he took in her bright purple platform heels. He was gripped by a sudden need to see her ass. He just knew it would be generously curvy, the type of ass a man liked to take his bare hand to as he forced her to cry for mercy.

"Turn around," he ordered, his voice husky with desire.

Her beautiful lips opened in surprise.

An image of her on her knees, smearing her perfect red lipstick on the column of his cock as he thrust it down her throat, flashed before him.

"I'm sorry. I didn't quite catch what you said."

Her voice was smooth and sweet. Dark honey.

"I said, sit down," he replied, trying to recover from his initial primal response to her presence.

"Oh! Yes, of course!"

She smoothed an arm under her skirt and perched on the edge of the seat. He could hear the faint rustle of her stockings as her legs brushed when she crossed them. With the way her skirt tightened over her slim thigh as she sat down, he could see just the barest outline of a garter. She was wearing thigh stockings, easier to access her…he ruthlessly cut off his own train of thought.

Michael laced his fingers together and rested his hands on the desk before him, mainly to prevent him from reaching out to grab her like some caveman. Christ, he had spent too long in the desert. It was like he didn't know how to behave around a beautiful woman anymore.

There was also something else about her…. It was at the back of his mind, if he could only focus on the matter at hand and not his cock's reaction to her presence.

"How can I help you, Mrs.—" He unconsciously held his breath, waiting for her to finish his sentence.

"It's Miss, actually."

He watched as she bit into the soft fullness of her bottom lip. *Christ, she was killing him!* The surge of possessive pleasure which hit his gut the moment she affirmed she was single certainly did not help. All he could think of was smacking that pert ass and making her scream with pleasure. Yeah, sick shit but a woman like this was made for kink.

"I'm not sure if you are the person I'm supposed to see. I was directed to this office, but when I told the lady out there that I was the new assistant professor, she just sort of sneered and a moment later hustled me in here."

"The new assistant professor of what?"

"Of English Literature."

Michael rifled through some papers in his inbox. "No. That can't be correct," he said as he pulled her application file from the stack. "I'm afraid there has been some mixup. That position was given to a Eustace Pringle."

He watched her grimace slightly before her red lips parted to say, "That would be me."

Michael's jaw tweaked to the right as he suppressed a smile. "You?"

"Me."

"You are *Eustace* Pringle?"

"It's a family name." She rushed on to say, "Actually I prefer Phoebe."

"Phoebe."

That name suited her far better. It fit the classic beauty. French sounding. Delicate.

He cleared his throat before continuing. "So you are Professor Phoebe Pringle?"

She nodded her head without speaking.

"How old are you?"

"I don't think you're allowed to ask me that."

"I'm asking anyway," he asserted.

Shifting in her seat, pushing her shoulders back as she tilted her chin up, she responded in an unmistakably stubborn tone, "I'm twenty-six." He loved a stubborn streak in a woman, it made for infinitely more occasions for creative punishments.

Still, there was something about her….

Fuck.

Michael looked down at the files on his desk regarding the murders. He just realized what it was that bothered him about her…besides the obvious. She matched the description of the two murder victims. Beautiful, mid-twenties, blonde.

As much as he would enjoy getting to know Phoebe, she had to go.

"Listen. This is a military academy full of men. I thought I was getting an old battle-ax who could take on a classroom filled with spirited, rowdy men. Not someone who… who…."

"Who what? Please do continue your incredibly sexist speech!"

There was that petulant stubborn streak again. The palm of his hand itched to feel the smooth skin of her ass.

He could see her eyes turn a bright shade of jade with her rising anger. The tiny silver charm on her necklace fluttered against the smooth column of her throat as she seethed. Damn him for an arrogant asshole but he wanted to see if he could push her a little further. He found her temper intoxicating, plus it served his purposes. He couldn't allow her to stay at the school.

But damn, her anger did something for him. Perhaps it was the thought of subduing her once she flew into a full passion. Grabbing her wrists, holding her body against his own as she twisted and raged to be set free. He shifted as he felt his cock respond to his wayward, highly unprofessional thoughts. The fabric of his uniform trousers became painful as it pinched and confined his thick shaft.

Michael rose to his full height, uncaring if she saw the evidence of his arousal. Placing his two fists on his desk, he leaned in close. *Christ.* Towering over her, he could just glimpse the soft swell of her breasts through her open neckline, could smell the sweet floral scent of her perfume.

Without another thought, he ground out, "Who looks like she should be bent over a desk instead of behind one."

The tense atmosphere in the room froze in stunned suspension.

There, that should do it, thought Michael. She would

sashay her gorgeous hips out of his office and back to wherever she came from. He felt a pang of remorse but it was for the best. He needed to focus on finding a murderer, not watching over the next possible victim.

There was just something about *this* particular woman. He felt like a marauding conqueror. The crude antecedents of his chosen profession. The men who went into battle and took what they wanted as spoils of war. Tossing a woman over his shoulder with a shout to his compatriots, 'this one is mine!' Michael clenched his jaw to prevent those very words from escaping his lips.

She slowly rose to her feet. Her pert little nose reached just below his jaw. Tilting her head back, she stormed, "How dare you say that to me? I am more than capable of leading a class of rowdy men, as you say, you… you… sexist… soldier!"

He responded out of habit. "Marine."

"What?" she asked, hands on hips. Her stance radiated righteous indignation. Her cheekbones were tinged with pink as her breath came in quick, angry gasps. Her green eyes were flashing. As he suspected, she was even more beautiful when she was in a rage. So much so that Michael was having a hard time regretting the rash words which antagonized her.

Leaning in closer, only the span of the desk protecting her from the full force of his body, the full force of his cock, he breathed almost against her mouth, "I said, I'm a Marine, babygirl, not a soldier."

He watched her lids lower to gaze at his mouth. Her tiny pink tongue caressed her lower lip, wetting it. Her gaze became liquid and unfocused. It was good to know he wasn't the only one feeling the pull of desire.

"What... what's the difference?" she whispered, her sweet, peppermint breath taunting him.

"Come a little closer and I'll show you."

Michael watched her sway slightly toward him at his command before giving herself a mental shake. Smoothing her hands down her skirt, he watched as she picked up her purse, holding it before her like a shield, and took a step back.

"Are you refusing me the position? Because I'm sure the members of the board who hired me would have a different opinion about that."

He bit his own tongue before replying that he wouldn't refuse her any position she liked.

Fuck. He needed as much autonomy here as possible. The last thing he needed was intervention from the board, many of whom did not know the real reason why he was chosen for the position, even if he was acting in the best interests of the primly sexy Professor Phoebe's safety.

"No," he responded through clenched teeth. "I'm not."

Phoebe nodded her head as she took another step back.

Michael straightened his back. His fists still clenched as he was forced to watch her retreat from him.

"Very well. Then I look forward to proving you wrong. Good day, Mr.—"

"It's Lieutenant Colonel Michael Lawson but you'll call me *Commander*." His voice rang with dark authority for now. Already vowing to hear those lips scream his name before the week was out. By the spark in her eye, he knew she hadn't missed the unspoken promise behind his order.

"Good day...." she paused. +-

He watched her lips open to address him as he bid. To recognize his authority over her, to *command her.*

"Good day," she said in a rush before turning and fleeing his office.

He was right. She had an amazing ass, and he was completely fucked.

At the very least, she just banished any concern he may have had for academy life competing with the excitement of battle.

Professor Phoebe Pringle may have just won this skirmish, but he was going to win the war and claim his prize.

CHAPTER 4

Phoebe walked in a daze behind the secretary, a Mrs. Lintz or Luds or something, as she showed Phoebe to her quarters. Most of the teaching staff stayed on campus in rooms similar to the dorm during term. It was tradition, droned on Mrs. L-something as she chatted about Phoebe needing to fill out some final paperwork and made more pronouncements on tradition and the way things were done at the school.

Phoebe barely missed crashing into the woman's back when she stopped in front of a heavy wooden door with a worn brass handle.

"Here you are, Professor Pringle."

"Call me Phoebe, please."

"No. It's tradition to call staff by their formal titles, Professor Pringle."

"Thank you, Mrs.…" said Phoebe genially as she held out her hand.

"Mrs. Ludtz," responded the woman crisply, disdainfully ignoring Phoebe's outstretched hand.

"Thank you, Mrs. Ludtz."

Phoebe took the woman's measure. Her severe demeanor and abrupt, judgmental way of talking gave the impression she was much older. Yet, upon closer inspection, Phoebe wouldn't put the woman past forty-five years old. Of course, the tight bun, bulky cardigan and serviceable shoes didn't help, thought Phoebe. Perhaps if the woman warmed to her, she would recommend a fun makeover. Phoebe always felt that a fabulous pair of shoes and the right shade of lipstick did wonders for a girl's outlook on life.

Mrs. Ludtz's sharp voice interrupted Phoebe's musings. "I have left a copy of your schedule and a map of the school grounds on your desk for you. Classes are over for the day but begin promptly at 8:00 am tomorrow. You have a meeting with the English Department head at 7:00 am. Most of the female staff are more mature and married, so, of course, they live off campus, so you are the only one housed here for the moment." The censure in the woman's voice was unmistakable.

It was with relief that Phoebe closed the door behind the disagreeable woman and leaned on it. Kicking off her high heels, she took two steps and face-planted onto the small, neatly-made twin bed. After a moment, she turned onto her back and stared sightlessly up at the ceiling.

What the hell had just happened?

Never in her life had she been spoken to that way. She honestly didn't think men still spoke to women like…like…that!

Good God!

The worse part of it all was instead of it causing a call

to arms from her inner feminine warrior it had made her feel, well, warm. Hot, really.

Good God!

And the way the man looked. She honestly didn't think men looked like… like… that!

He was a marble statue of a Roman centurion come to life. All chiseled jaw and harsh, beautiful angles. Those strong shoulders! The way he looked in his blue uniform. His short haircut only emphasized his high cheekbones and beautiful, deep blue eyes. And when he spoke, his voice was dark and commanding, as if he was used to everyone in the room standing there just waiting to obey his every utterance.

He was arrogant. Condescending. An ass. A sexist Marine.

He was also tall. And handsome. And…sexy as fuck. The kind of man who grabbed you by the hair to tilt your head back for a kiss. Who took what he wanted without asking.

Good God. She was fucked.

Phoebe gave herself another mental shake. No. She had an assignment to complete. The owner of the newspaper was watching her on this one. She needed to stay focused. She needed to remember why she was here.

She needed to stay far away from Lieutenant Colonel Michael Lawson.

* * *

PHOEBE SURVEYED THE ROOM. She had interviewed people in prison who'd had a cozier cell than this. The room was spartan to say the least, containing only the bare necessities. The room looked to be as old as the university itself. Even the windows had that distorted wobble of turn-of-the-century glass. Apparently, even the teachers were subjected to rigid military conditions.

Ah, well. At least it had a private bathroom and shower and it was only for a week or two, enough time for her to poke around and see what she could learn about the suspicious deaths without rousing suspicion herself.

Now that she had passed the first crucial test and was accepted as an assistant professor, it was time to tackle the gruesome task of looking through the files Henry had provided. They contained information and photos of the women as well as the autopsy reports and photos. Phoebe had delayed doing this necessary part until she was certain she could infiltrate the school. No point in upsetting herself if, in the end, she couldn't write the story.

Sitting cross-legged on the bed, Phoebe opened her laptop and took out the two files on the murdered women.

Opening the first one, she was startled to see a striking resemblance to herself.

Ms. Annie Porter had honey blonde hair and favored red lipstick judging by both her photo in the file as well as the social media profile that was still up and that Phoebe was flipping through. She'd been only twenty years old and the girlfriend of one of the midshipmen when she was found naked and strangled. According to the autopsy report, there was nothing sexual about her murder. As Phoebe continued to read, her hand flew to her mouth in shock. Oh God!

Phoebe quickly grabbed the other file. Again noticing a strong resemblance to her own features, she flipped to the autopsy report for Mary Bruen, the professor she had just replaced. It had the same horrible note.

Both women had been strangled.

Both were found naked with a strange, somewhat satanic symbol carved into their chests.

Neither was sexually assaulted.

Both had their livers removed; the organs were not recovered at the scene.

Phoebe shuddered as images of every Jack the Ripper documentary she had ever seen plagued her.

It was one thing to report on a murder.

It was another when both women bore an uncomfortable resemblance to yourself, and yet quite another when it was assumed the murderer carved out and ate each woman's liver!

She needed a break, and a stiff drink.

Putting aside her own research for the night, Phoebe looked her schedule over and started to jot down some notes for a lesson plan. She would have to play the game of being Professor Pringle if she wanted to last long enough to find out the truth about the deaths of those two poor women! And the thought that word would get back to Michael about what an amazing, competent teacher she was didn't even cross her mind... nope... not even once.

* * *

AFTER WORKING LATE into the night, Phoebe stripped off her clothes and finally fell on top of the bed, dressed only in her panties, too exhausted to put on pajamas. Sleep did not come easily though. Visions of a tall, uniformed Marine forcing her to bend over his desk swam before her eyes. She bit her lip and moaned as she imagined him tearing her skirt off and kicking her feet wide to position his own hips behind her. She could hear the sound of him lowering his zipper as if he were really in the room. Her hand drifted across her flat stomach to rest between her thighs. Dipping her fingers beneath the edge of her panties, she raised her knees up. She imagined the scrape from the fabric of his uniform against her soft skin as he stepped closer. The feel of his large, warm hands on her hips as he held her down. Could feel the press of his cock against her pussy.

Phoebe's fingers moved in swift circles over her clit. Faster and faster. Increasing the pressure. Her hips rising off the bed.

He thrust forward. Impaling her. So thick and big she cried out from the pain of the intrusion.

Phoebe squeezed her eyes closed as she let out a soft keen in the silent room. Coming to the thought of Michael forcing himself on her.

Lowering her hips, she haphazardly tossed a corner of the blanket over her body, thoughts of an arrogant Marine lulling her into a restive sleep.

* * *

PHOEBE SAT UP IN BED, looking about the quiet, unfamiliar room, unsure of what had just woken her.

She stopped to listen.

Nothing.

Conscious of her undressed state, she reached over to her open suitcase and grabbed a pair of yoga pants and a T-shirt. Slipping them on, feeling more secure, she turned to burrow under the covers.

There it was again.

The sound of approaching footsteps just outside her door. A heavy footfall. She glanced at her phone. Three am. She could see through the shaft of light under the door that someone was standing just outside.

Waiting.

Phoebe held her breath.

Her eyes grew wide as the doorknob slowly turned. Then stopped.

Thank God she had remembered to lock the door.

The footsteps paced away, only to return again.

This time whoever it was rattled the doorknob angrily. The door itself shook.

Phoebe covered her mouth to prevent a scream from escaping.

Who the hell was trying to get into her room? Mrs. Ludtz had made it clear she was the only person down this particular hallway. After studying the map, she had learned the male students were housed in a completely different building across campus.

Could it be Michael, she thought wildly.

Fantasy was one thing, but she wasn't prepared for matching wits, and other things, with him just now.

Just as she was about to risk yelling 'go away,' the person stormed off.

Phoebe wrapped the thin blanket from the bed around her shoulders and sat against the headboard.

So much for sleeping, she thought as her eyes stayed focused on the door.

Standing up on shaking legs, she slowly made her way to the door. She stopped and unplugged the bedside lamp and held it up like a weapon. Stepping closer, she pressed her ear to the wood panel and listened intently. There wasn't a sound. Unclenching her left fist, she reached for the doorknob. Twisting the lock, she threw the door open quickly while taking a defensive step back, raising the lamp high and at the ready.

The hallway was empty.

Placing her hand on the door to steady her shaking limbs, she poked her head out and looked left and right. Nothing.

It was then she became aware her hand was sticky and wet. Pulling it off the door, she looked down.

Her hand was covered in what looked like blood.

Crying out, she fell back against the wall. Holding her hand up to the light in the hallway, she examined it more closely. The sticky substance on her palm was a bright red. Phoebe sniffed the air.

It *was* blood.

She then turned her attention to the door. The image was smeared, probably because it was painted in haste, but unmistakable. It was a satanic symbol. The same image that had been carved into the chests of both murdered women. A crude, simplistic image of a goat over a pentagram.

It was an unmistakable warning.

Swallowing the bile in her throat, Phoebe quickly wet a towel and cleaned off the symbol. She couldn't risk

RECKLESS SURRENDER

raising an alarm on campus. The commander already wanted her gone. This would give him the perfect excuse to force her to leave. No, she would tell no one. This only proved she was on to something. Phoebe was determined to see her investigation through.

When she was finished, she closed the door, this time throwing the small deadbolt lock as well.

* * *

UNDAUNTED, Phoebe walked into her classroom at a quarter to eight the next morning. It was a pleasant, cozy room. Something straight out of *Dead Poet's Society* with its dusty old bookshelves and lattice window overlooking a slightly overgrown courtyard. She loved it. It made her feel like she should be wearing tweed and smoking a pipe.

The meeting with the department head had gone surprisingly well. Professor Jones was a short, pleasant man who was shockingly candid.

"Listen. They are here to learn about the Navy. That is all they care about. And all the Navy cares about is that they learn about the Navy...and perhaps some math. English is fairly low on everyone's priority list. I need you to make sure they know the basics. Shakespeare, Dickens, Hemingway. Just enough culture befitting an officer. Got it?" said Professor Jones as he shoved papers into a worn leather satchel. Phoebe followed him down the hall as he shuffled along to his first class.

"What have they learned so far this year?" she asked as she tried to keep up in her platform heels.

"Nothing. The last teacher we hired quit less than a

week in, unable to…well there was some unpleasantness and since then the class has been a quiet study hall. Good luck, Professor Pringle. Your classroom is right down this hall, third door on the left."

Knowing he had just given her the perfect in, Phoebe asked, "What sort of unpleasantness? I hope it had nothing to do with cheating or plagiarism?"

Professor Jones stopped mid-shuffle and turned to her. Without looking up, and nervously adjusting the buckle on his satchel, he said, "No, no, no. Nothing like that. They have an honor code here and they take it very seriously. It was…well…a few weeks ago…two lovely young women were…well they were found murdered in the forest that borders the school."

Phoebe laid a consoling hand on his upper arm. "That is terrible. I'm so sorry. Did you know the women?"

"One of them was a teacher in my department. The other was a girlfriend of one of the men on campus. The boy was cleared of course. He was training on a boat out in the bay at the time of the murder."

At that, Professor Jones seemed to come back to himself, giving Phoebe a startled look as if in his reminiscences he had forgotten she was standing there.

"I've said too much. It was probably some vagrant passing through. Don't believe what they say about it being someone on campus. That's just speculation from the locals."

"You mean they didn't catch the murderer?" Phoebe, of course, knew they had not, but she always felt it was best to plead ignorance when ferreting out information.

"Don't let any of it frighten you away, Miss Pringle. I'm sure the school is safe despite the strange circumstances… well…yes…I'm sure we are all safe." And then he was gone.

Turned out Henry and Jimmy were right, there was a story here and this school was so frazzled and distracted no one seemed to care if she could spell Shakespeare let alone teach it.

Phoebe couldn't wait to get back to her room to start her research. There was more to these murders than just the sensational aspects. She was sure of it.

* * *

Laying out her lesson plan notes, she leaned against the desk and waited for the first bell. Her first class of the day was with third class students. She wasn't sure if that meant they were sophomores or juniors but she would read up on that later. She hadn't really had time to learn the ins and outs of military academy life.

At precisely 7:55 am, students began to quietly file in. Phoebe had expected a little more of the noise and chaos typical of college students. These men were calm and orderly as they took their seats and patiently waited for her to begin. Instinctively realizing that exact timing was probably important on this campus, she nervously watched the clock hands till it was precisely 8:00 am before beginning.

Standing upright, she addressed the class. "Good morning, students!"

Several hands immediately shot up.

What the hell, thought Phoebe. What could I have possibly gotten wrong so quickly?

She nodded her head toward the student closest to her.

"With all due respect, ma'am. We are midshipmen, not students."

At her confused look, another voice chimed in, "We are considered ensigns in the Navy, ma'am. A low ranking officer," he clarified. "So we are technically midshipmen in the Navy, not just college students."

"Shut up! That is so freakin' cool!" she exclaimed.

The whole class laughed and the tension eased.

She introduced herself and then asked the class to one by one stand and introduce themselves. After the greetings were finished, she announced they would be studying Shakespeare. There were small, but perceptible, groans.

"What? Are you remembering the Shakespeare plays you were forced to read in high school? *Romeo and Juliet*. *Hamlet*. You don't think Shakespeare applies to your military career? That a few men strutting around in tights have nothing in common with you?" asked Phoebe, her hands on her hips.

"With all due respect, ma'am, yes," someone from the back of the classroom responded.

Perhaps it was the *Dead Poets Society* vibe, but she felt compelled to inspire these men. Pulling out the wooden straight-back chair from behind her desk, she hitched her skirt up and stepped onto the seat. Raising her arm up high, she shouted, "'Cowards die but many deaths, the valiant taste of death but once!'"

"Hooyah!" erupted the whole class, reciting the naval battle cry in unison.

"'Cry havoc and let slip the dogs of war!'" she growled with aplomb.

"Hooyah!" they all cried out with enthusiasm as they beat their fists on their desks.

"Yes! Yes!" she clapped. "Those are from Shakespeare's *Julius Caesar*! Now let me see…. Oh! I have a good one." Lowering her voice to sound more masculine, she cried out, "'From now until the end of the world, we and it shall be remembered. We few, we Band of Brothers. For he…'"

Phoebe broke off with a start as Michael strolled into the room, looking like the embodiment of authority and command in his dress blue uniform.

"I, ah… I…"

"Finish the quote, Professor Pringle, you're on a roll!" called out one of the midshipmen.

"Yes, please, Professor Pringle, finish what you were doing," said Michael, his dark gaze direct and scrutinizing.

At the sound of his voice, the whole classroom stood at attention.

"At ease, men."

The students, that is the midshipmen, all sat.

All the while, Phoebe was desperately trying to see how she could get down from her chair with any dignity. In her excitement to rally the men she hadn't really thought her plan through. Her red skirt wasn't so much tight as it was form fitting. While only having to hitch it up to mid-calf to step onto the chair, Phoebe was afraid she would have to hike it up a great deal higher to get *off* the chair. And there was no way she was going to be able to do it and keep her heels on. Carefully, she slipped out of one shoe, grimacing when it thunked as it fell to the floor. She quickly slipped out of the other. She lost several inches of tactical height in the maneuver, but she had no choice.

Michael strolled down the aisle between the desks. "Professor Pringle, please don't let me interrupt your lesson." He moved to lean against the wall directly to her right.

Recovering some of her dignity, Phoebe swallowed hard and tried to remember the line. "'We few, we Band of Brothers. For he who sheds his blood with me shall be my brother.'"

Casting a nervous glance toward Michael, she asked, "Who can tell me what play that is from? Anyone?"

After a long pause, Michael chimed in.

"I think I can answer for my men. *King Henry the Fifth*," said Michael with a knowing smile.

The bell rang before Phoebe could reply. *Saved by the bell*, she thought. Trying to act like she meant to be standing on a chair shouting like a banshee, she called out, "Read the first act of *Henry the Fifth* for class on Wednesday."

The men all filed out with respectful nods toward Michael and murmured 'Good afternoon, Commander' as they went.

Soon the classroom was empty.

Save for Michael.

Leaning against the wall.

And her.

Standing on her chair.

Phoebe kept her eyes forward, hoping, as if by sheer will, she could make him leave. She could hear the rustle of his uniform coat as he straightened up from the wall. Then the sound of his booted heels on the hardwood floor.

One step. Another.

Memories of her sleepless night came back to her. The heavy footfall outside her door. Had it been him?

He was standing to her side. Even up on the chair, her five-feet-four inches without her heels was nothing compared to his obviously over six-feet frame.

"Phoebe."

"Yes," she whispered, looking down at her nervously twitching fingers. She wished she knew how this man could make her feel like an errant school girl. Strike that…she knew why.

"Yes, what?" he ground out.

At that she turned her head to look at him. They were almost eye-level with the help of the chair. With a start, she realized he was angry. The polite nonchalance he had shown to the class had just been a facade. It was there in the set of his jaw. The rigid line of his brow. The cold look in his blue eyes.

"I asked you a question and I expect an answer." Each word was clipped as if his sharp teeth were biting them off at the ends.

Flustered, Phoebe demurred. "Yes, sir?" Holding her breath to see if that was the right answer. In her very short acquaintance with this man, it was clear he was not a man to be crossed or angered.

Or lied to, she thought with a flush.

Good God! She briefly wondered if New York being only a couple hundred miles away from Buzzards Bay was far enough to run when he learned of her true purpose here.

"Do you mind telling me what you thought you were doing climbing up on this chair? In high heels no less?"

There it was again. It was something in his tone. The harsh schoolmaster. Each question only missing the 'young lady' tacked onto the end.

Unbidden, almost against her will, she looked at the desk in front of them. Phoebe imagined herself bent over it.

Dressed in a schoolgirl's uniform, the worn wood cool beneath her fingertips. He easily flips up her short, plaid skirt, exposing the creamy skin of her ass and her hot pink thong. Pacing around the desk, Michael methodically slaps a long, wooden ruler against his palm as he repeats a litany of the rules she has broken. She bounces up on her toes as her anxiety increases, knowing the punishment will be severe. She can feel him behind her. A warm hand cups the curve of her right buttock. He warns her the punishment will be painful, moments before the ruler strikes high on her cheeks. She cries out in pain but he doesn't stop. One strike for every broken rule. The thin strip of wood warms her skin. Stinging hot pinpricks run over her ass to the tops of her thighs. Her stomach clenches in between each punishing blow. Finally, he places the ruler on the desk. It's time for your real punishment, he says as he frees his thick cock.

"Phoebe, once again, I have asked you a question you have failed to promptly answer."

Phoebe blinked as she brought Michael back into focus, the schoolgirl fantasy still whispering through her mind. Her cheeks flushed as she realized her nipples were tight with arousal.

"I... ah... well... it was a *Dead Poet's* thing," she stammered, as she pivoted to see if she could somehow step down and put some distance between herself and him.

"Stop fidgeting, you are going to fall."

He wrapped his arm around her hips just below her ass and lifted her off the chair. Phoebe had no choice but to put her hands on his shoulders as she murmured protests and complaints.

Slowly. Impossibly slowly.

He slid her down the length of his front till her stockinged feet touched the ground. Without her heels, the top of her head barely reached his shoulder. She could smell the musky spice of his cologne. Feel the strength of the muscles across his chest. He radiated heat and energy. Even the brass buttons on his uniform felt warm beneath her fingers.

Her cheeks flamed, hoping the heavy wool of his coat would prevent him from feeling the evidence of her own arousal as her breasts brushed his front.

She was robbed of speech. Keeping her eyes trained forward, she waited for him to remove his hand from her lower back. Instead, he pressed her forward slightly. It was a light but masterful touch. Just enough to have her stomach brush the hard ridge of his cock. He placed a finger under her chin and forced her to meet his gaze.

"'Among the many lovely things, that make the magic of her face. Among the beauties, black and rose, that make her body's charm and grace.'" He spoke soft and low.

Baudelaire. He was reciting Baudelaire's *The Temptation* to her.

Here he was, this big, scary Marine, reciting a love poem. Phoebe felt lightheaded.

His presence. His anger. Her fantasy. Her lies.

It was all spinning about in her head like fluttering butterflies on fast forward.

"Listen carefully, baby. You ever… ever… get up on a chair like that again. Perching dangerously on the seat in high heels. Displaying this delicious body of yours to my men…"

Phoebe started to object but the press of his hand against her lower back silenced her.

"Displaying your body to my men," he repeated. "I really will bend you over this desk and tan that magnificent ass of yours with my belt till you cry for mercy."

Here he was, this big, scary Marine who recites poetry…and reads minds!

Phoebe just knew her cheeks were flushed a bright scarlet.

Boldly, she admonished, "I don't think you are allowed to say such things to me."

"I did anyway," he responded as a single fingertip ran down the curve of her heated cheek. "Change your mind about leaving yet?"

Phoebe stubbornly raised her chin as her eyes narrowed on him assessingly. "Nope."

There was a clamoring in the hall as the next class of midshipmen began to enter.

Michael stepped back. Phoebe felt oddly bereft without the support of his hand on her back.

She watched almost in slow motion as he leaned forward, his head tilted down toward her face.

In one crazy, wanton moment she thought he was going to kiss her, right here in the middle of the classroom, in front of the students… er… midshipmen.

Instead his lips grazed her ear as he whispered, "I suggest you put your shoes back on."

And with that, he was gone.

Phoebe stood there for a moment. Trying to come to terms with what was reality and what was fantasy. He disappeared so quickly she could almost believe she had imagined the whole thing. As she numbly turned to put on her shoes, she recalled the poem he'd recited. *The Temptation*.

With a start, she recalled the opening lines. *The Demon, in my chamber high. This morning came to visit me. And, thinking he would find some fault, He whispered, "I would know of thee."*

Had it been Michael at her door last night? Was it Michael who had put the satanic symbol on her door as a warning to leave?

Phoebe shivered despite the warmth of the classroom.

CHAPTER 5

"It's beautiful."

Keeping her balance on the rounded wet rocks, Phoebe looked out over the bay. She was with Amber, an assistant professor from the math department, who had suggested the early morning walk. Amber was short and plump in all the right places with curly, mousy brown hair and a sweet smile. She'd taken an instant liking to Phoebe, glad to have another female under the age of fifty on the campus. She had made it her mission to see that Phoebe was acclimated and happy in her new position. Phoebe felt a pang of guilt for deceiving such a kind and open person but reminded herself that her motives were good. It seemed the whole campus was divided into two camps about the murders. Those who practically denied they had occurred and those who wanted to gossip about all the gruesome details. No one seemed fired up to actually catch the killer.

Everyone bought into the assumption some deranged homeless man just happened to wander into the area, kill two women over the course of three weeks and wander out. The fact that such a man would stick out like sore thumb in such a small, tightly-knit community and yet was never observed, didn't seem to bother anyone. As far as she could tell, Phoebe was the only one actually trying to seek justice for the slain women.

"I thought you might like the view," observed Amber.

Focusing back on the present, Phoebe nodded as she took a sip of her mocha latte. Her warmed breath created misty swirls of white each time she breathed. The view was stunning in its raw beauty. Large rocks gave way to smooth white sand beaches which were buffeted by surprisingly strong waves. It was difficult to tell where the slate gray water ended and the gray sky began. Only the faintest glow of soft pink on the horizon hinted at a sunrise. A few boats were braving the harsh winds as they maneuvered around the peninsula where the spider-like lighthouse perched.

They had stopped at an adorable cafe to grab coffee drinks and some pastries before following the path between the military academy grounds and the woods to the shoreline of the bay.

Phoebe loved the sights and smells. The late fall morning had an icy crispness to the air. Feeding off the energy of the woods and the churning waters of the bay, everything felt alive and invigorating to her. So different from the stale, rank smells of the city with its crush of harried people.

"Oh my God! You have to try this raspberry preserve croissant," raved Amber.

Phoebe gingerly took the buttery pastry from Amber.

Holding it by its wax paper wrapping, she bit into the warm and crusty bread. A burst of tart sweetness hit her tongue as she also moaned her appreciation. A small dollop of raspberry preserves had escaped the pastry from the side and dripped onto the corner of her mouth. The tip of her tongue poked out to sweep the delicate treat from her lips just as she saw him.

Emerging from the forest's edge like some mythical beast, he was all hard muscle and harsh angles. Dressed only in dark blue sweat shorts, his naked chest was on full display. Despite the chill, a fine sheen of sweat made his skin glisten in the early morning light. It was entrancing to watch the fluid motion of his body as he ran. Although distance separated them, Phoebe was drawn into the intense scrutiny of his gaze. Alarmed, she watched as he slowed his pace and headed toward them.

Amber gasped. "Holy fuck. He's coming this way! Jesus Christ, he's built."

Phoebe had actually forgotten Amber was by her side.

They became aware that he had a white T-shirt fisted in his hand when Michael pulled it over his head to cover his wide chest and flat stomach. Phoebe ruthlessly stifled a disappointed groan.

"Ladies." Although he greeted them both with a nod, his eyes stayed glued on Phoebe.

"Good morning, Commander," said Amber.

Phoebe just stared.

Amber elbowed her in the side.

"Good morning," she softly uttered. There was a noticeable pause after her simple greeting. She watched his jaw harden and an unmistakable glint appear in his sharp eyes at her staunch refusal to call him Commander. There was something too charged in the term. Too sexual, as if she were submitting to him. Phoebe clenched her thighs at the tingling sensation caused by her wayward thoughts.

"You ladies should not be out here alone. This area can be dangerous."

His voice was dark and low…commanding, like the schoolmaster he was. Once more the schoolgirl fantasy floated across her heated mind.

"Thank you, Commander. We were just heading back to the campus," responded Amber.

"Good. I would hate to see either of you harmed."

Phoebe just stared.

Amber once again elbowed her in the side.

Phoebe could only nod, still transfixed. It annoyed her how his presence affected her. He was just so male!

As Amber bent down to stuff her now-empty coffee cup in her backpack, Michael took a step toward Phoebe. Tilting her head back because of his superior height, she noticed how his dark blue eyes appeared almost black in the weak morning light. He reached out and stroked the edge of her mouth with the pad of his thumb. Her own lips parted as he raised the thumb to his mouth and licked.

Michael then leaned in to whisper in her ear, "You taste sweet, babygirl."

Until that moment, Phoebe had not realized it was possible for a person's heart to stop from a rush of desire. She felt as though she may never breathe again. She didn't know if the endearment was a reference to her diminutive height or if it had a deeper, more sexually charged promise. Either way, it made her feel weak.

Taking a step back before Amber noticed their interaction, he said, "You ladies have a *pleasurable* morning." His eyes were once again only for Phoebe.

They both watched as Michael turned and ran back along the path, into the forest.

"I'd play headmaster and naughty schoolgirl with him any day," quipped Amber.

Phoebe's cheeks heated as her new friend mentioned the precise fantasy she herself had been having about Michael…every damn night.

"Come on. We'll be late for our classes." Phoebe grabbed her own backpack and they followed the shore to get back onto the walkway which would take them to campus.

After walking in silence for a few minutes, Amber shivered and quickened her step. "We shouldn't have taken this way."

"Why? Isn't this the quicker path back to campus?"

"Yeah, but this place gives me the creeps," responded Amber as she motioned with her head to the right.

There was a small clearing between the edge of the woods and the beginning of the shore. Despite the gorgeous golden and crimson hues of the trees about them, there was one which stood out in stark relief. Its gnarled and twisted branches were bare. The thick trunk of the tree was marred with black scorch marks. At its base was a massive rock. Its top was smooth and flat, and along the edges there were numerous strange carvings. It was impossible not to feel a sense of foreboding.

"What is it?"

"It's called the witch's tree but legend has it that it's where they burned the Mad Monk."

A chill crept down Phoebe's spine.

"It's also where they found those two poor women," continued Amber.

"They found them here?" asked Phoebe as she slipped her phone from her pocket. Turning her body slightly, she kept the phone low to her hip as she tried to secretly snap photos of the place and the carvings etched into the rock's worn surface. If she wasn't mistaken, several of the carvings resembled the symbol painted in blood on her door. The same symbol carved into the murder victims' chests.

"Yeah. It was awful. The whole campus is still shaken by it."

"Did you know them?"

Amber shook her head no. Leaning in, she whispered, "I heard the evil bastard who did it carved a pentagram on their breasts and left them naked on top of the rock. What kind of sick bastard would do such a thing?"

Before Phoebe could answer, they heard a soft mournful tune on the wind. If Amber hadn't grabbed her by the arm and inched closer, Phoebe would have thought she'd imagined it. She listened intently. There, just above the sound of the crashing surf. A child's voice. Singing. It sounded like *Rock-a-Bye-Baby* but the words were wrong. As they listened, a figure appeared. It was a female with a coarsely woven blanket draped about her shoulders. Her hair hung in wild, tangled waves about her shoulders.

Wee little fingers, eyes are shut tight
Now dead asleep - never again to see light

Amber huffed in disgust and quickly dragged Phoebe away. As Phoebe struggled to keep up with the other woman's marching steps, she cried out, "Hold up, Amber. Who was that?"

"Fucking Loony Ludtz," Amber snorted.

"That was Mrs. Ludtz?" Phoebe was incredulous. The figure was some ways off but still, it didn't resemble the extremely restrained, pinned up woman she was accustomed to seeing scowling about campus.

"I don't know if *Mrs.* applies any longer," sneered Amber.

As they quickened their steps back to the safety and relative sanity of campus, Amber regaled Phoebe with the story of Mrs. Ludtz's recent failed marriage. Apparently after learning her husband had been cheating on her with a much younger woman a few months ago, she had become unhinged. For a month she wore only unrelenting black to mourn the death of her marriage. Then she disappeared into the woods for over a week claiming she needed to go back to nature to find herself. When she returned to school, Ludtz started to chastise and verbally abuse any of the female staff who wore makeup or high heels, which explained her instant dislike of Phoebe.

"Her latest craziness is to claim her Indian heritage is demanding she cleanse the area after the murders."

Phoebe didn't know what singing an old nursery rhyme had to do with the local Indian culture, but she kept that to herself.

"Why does Michael… er… I mean the Lieutenant Colonel keep her on staff?"

Amber shrugged her shoulders. "He's new to the position and Ludtz knows this school like the back of her hand. She wasn't anyone's friend before this but people still feel sorry for her. Besides, I'd much rather he focused on Drake and Casey than Mrs. Ludtz's marriage problems."

"Who are Drake and Casey?"

"You mean no other teacher has warned you about those two midshipmen?"

Phoebe shook her head, trying to picture her roster to remember if she had them in her class. "No, why?"

"Rumor has it they were suspects in the murders before they announced it was that homeless man no one can find."

Phoebe was about to comment that she hadn't seen their names mentioned in any of the articles she had read, but she didn't want to clue Amber in on the fact that she was interested in or researching the murders.

"No!" she exclaimed with appropriate shock and horror.

Amber's eyes were lit with gruesome excitement. "They both have an odd way about them, always getting written up for something or other, and they were caught trying to cut up a dead squirrel. You know what they say about people who kill and torture animals." Amber nodded her head sagely.

Phoebe made a mental note to look into both Drake and Casey. She remembered Henry's theory of the crime, that some rich politician's son was actually behind the murders and was being protected because of their parents' influence. She wondered if Drake or Casey had powerful parents. The only way to find out conclusively was to look in the student files. Unlike a regular school, Puller Academy would have extensive information on the parents' backgrounds and professions. She might also learn more about the boys through their disciplinary records.

The only problem was, the files were guarded over by Loony Ludtz, and her office was right outside of Michael's.

It was like some kind of macabre game, thought Phoebe with a wry smile.

You are trapped in Buzzards Bay.

Your goal is to get past the lunatic and fight the scary powerful king to learn the secret behind the mad monk murders.

Be careful not to fall under the king's seductive spell or you may lose your life!

Good lord! Perhaps the monk wasn't the only one who was mad around here.

CHAPTER 6

"What about the blood?"

"It will be messy but I think it will be worth it in the end."

Standing outside her classroom door later that same morning, Phoebe listened to the conversation of the midshipmen inside, horrified. After leaving Amber, she had raced to change and make it to her first class. Thoughts of the witch's tree and that ominous rock clouded her mind, competing with thoughts of murder and satanic symbols, and now this!

"I want to hear it scream, like really scream."

Phoebe dropped her shoulder bag and turned to run down the hallway. She needed to find Michael. Now was not the time to wonder why her first thought was to run to Michael for help. At this very moment, all she *could* think about was running to him for help. He was big and strong and honorable and she wanted to feel his protective presence while they decided how to proceed.

"Professor Pringle."

Stopping, she hazarded a look over her shoulder. "Yes?" she asked, her voice sounding weak and hesitant.

"I see you overheard our plans. You might as well come in and hear all the gory details."

The midshipman picked up her shoulder bag and waited, expecting her to follow. Taking a deep breath, knowing she would never be able to outrun the midshipman, she had no choice but to enter the classroom. All the men turned as she walked in.

"Professor Pringle, you are just in time. Do you have any good quotes from Shakespeare about murder or death?" asked Thomas.

"Men, whatever it is you're planning—"

"I don't think Shakespeare would be appropriate. It should be something from a Native American author," offered Chris.

"No. You both have it wrong. It has to be something from the Bible, that makes more sense," piped up Joe.

Several classmates called out their agreement to Joe's idea.

Phoebe couldn't take it a moment longer. Without another thought to her own safety, she cried out, "You have to stop! Please! You can't do this!"

"But, Professor Pringle, it's tradition," complained Thomas.

"Tradition! Murder is tradition?" *What the hell had she gotten herself into?*

"Well, yeah," said Chris. "Every twenty-fifth of October."

Raising her hands protectively in front of her, Phoebe took a step back. This was insane. This couldn't be true. "You murder someone every twenty-fifth of October?"

"Well, in effigy," corrected Joe.

"You are all mad. You need hel— Wait. What?"

"We murder someone in effigy. The Mad Monk."

* * *

Forcing them all to close their eyes, Phoebe took a quick swig from the flask of whiskey she kept in her shoulder bag. It had been a gift from Henry. He said every true journalist should always have something strong on hand to help a source loosen their tongue when necessary. It also came in handy for other things… like thinking your entire class was involved in a heinous murder plot.

After getting over her shock, Phoebe learned the details of the Mad Monk tradition.

* * *

The Order of Saint John monks arrived in Buzzards Bay in the spring of 1665 to convert the Wampanoag, the local tribe of Algonquian Indians, to Christianity. In the fall of 1666, Brother Phineas and Brother Godfrey headed deep into the thick woods to seek out the winter camp of the tribe. Although misguided, they thought they were doing God's work by converting the 'savages.'

They never arrived at the camp.

Weeks later, Brother Phineas was found, naked and covered in blood, crouching over the partially consumed body of Brother Godfrey. Phineas' emaciated appearance and wild ravings led the tribe's shaman to declare he had become a wendigo, an evil spirit. Mythos among the Algonquian was that anyone who became lost in the woods and resorted to cannibalism forfeited all their humanity. They became violent creatures who brought death and decay with them along with an insatiable hunger for more human flesh. The only way to kill the evil spirit was to burn the wendigo alive and scatter its ashes to the four winds.

Brother Phineas, or the human shell of the man he once was, was seized by the Wampanoag. After burning him alive, his charred body was placed on the large rock in front of the tree now called the witch's tree, the bones pulverized into dust and scattered.

It didn't work.

The monk's evil spirit continued to roam the woods at night on the anniversary of his death, claiming victims.

The legend of the Mad Monk was born.

Eventually, even the colonists began to fear the annual return of the monk's evil spirit. So every twenty-fifth of October they began to recreate the shaman's ceremonial killing of the wendigo by burning an effigy of the Mad Monk. When the military took over the monastery in the early nineteen hundreds and converted it to the Puller Academy, the midshipmen kept up the local tradition.

Dressing in black robes and carrying torches, they ran into the woods to chase each other around. The idea being they were scaring the evil spirit, corralling it toward the waiting effigy. Then at midnight, they would light the specially prepared bonfire, complete with a stuffed dummy perched on top to represent the Mad Monk.

Apparently, it was quite the celebration on campus and the highlight of the fall term. Their Halloween, really.

This year the midshipmen were planning on using a more realistic dummy with a cheap speaker placed in its chest so it sounded as if the dummy were screaming in pain.

One of the midshipmen approached the blackboard where he drew a strange symbol. "We are going to paint this on the dummy. Isn't it awesome?"

Phoebe couldn't believe her eyes. It was the symbol carved on both women's chests. The one the police file said was a pentagram, a satanic symbol. She had always had her doubts but had not been able to find anything on the internet that more closely resembled the symbol. "What does it represent?"

"It's the Wampanoag's symbol for a wendigo."

And the symbol left on her door a couple nights ago.

CHAPTER 7

Phoebe quickly sprinted across the damp and chilly quad, careful not to slip on the slick flagstone path. She needed to see those student files and then get to the library to research the wendigo symbol. Her time was running out. Soon someone was bound to learn she wasn't actually a professor named Pringle. There was no use denying she was worried about one person in particular, one handsome, arrogant, sexy-as-fuck person.

Speaking of Michael, some of the teachers had thrown an impromptu welcome lunch for her in one of the outlying buildings. She had overheard Amber complain she couldn't get in to see the commander until the following morning because he was off-campus at a meeting all afternoon.

It was an opportunity she didn't want to pass up.

These teachers were all so sweet and welcoming, Phoebe felt a twinge of guilt for lying to them, using them for information. It was strange; she hadn't felt guilty when she took down the King of Chinatown or that time she spent working the front desk of the gym chain to expose their coercive contract practices.

This just felt…different. She was actually *enjoying* being a teacher. She had forgotten how much fun it was to share her love of literature with someone. The debates on hidden meaning and symbolism. Chatting about the world events that were taking place at the time of writing that may have impacted the manuscript. The challenge of coming up with material that would engage and excite the midshipmen.

She was also learning all about the fascinating hierarchy and rigid class system of the school. The fourth class were actually what she would call freshmen. First class were the seniors. It was daunting to learn that many would graduate and launch straight into a military career. The men chatted animatedly about what it would take to be accepted into the naval flight training program or signing their '2 for 7s.' This was apparently a commitment document the Navy or Marines had each man in his second class sign upon entering his third class, or junior year, committing to two more years of school and then five years of military service. When Phoebe thought back on what she was thinking about during her junior year in college, she grimaced. Let's just say it didn't come close to committing her life to protecting her country. There were even rumors buzzing about campus of making the academy co-ed. The men, as would be expected, were excited over the possible change.

It also gave her a whole new respect for Michael. She had learned over the last few days that he was a celebrated graduate of the Puller Military Academy and apparently one of the youngest Lieutenant Colonels in the Marines. The midshipmen talked with reverence whenever they mentioned the *Commander*. She had heard about his hair-raising battles in Afghanistan and close calls during two tours in Iraq. The men he had saved. The villages he had helped. The difference he had made in the world. Here she thought she was doing her part taking down corrupt business owners, and in a small way she was, but that was nothing compared to what he had done.

It also helped Phoebe understand his demeanor toward her. It didn't excuse it, her inner feminine warrior harrumphed in a fit of pique, but it did help her understand it.

This was a man of focus, of determination. A man who did what needed to be done. *Who took what he wanted. Who was accustomed to being obeyed.*

* * *

"Good morning, Mrs. Ludtz," Phoebe said with false cheer, watching the older woman closely. Phoebe wasn't sure if Mrs. Ludtz recognized her as one of the people on the shore who had witnessed her strange behavior the other day. If she did, it would make Phoebe's task all that much harder. Mrs. Ludtz barely spared Phoebe a glance before returning to her typing.

Well, that answers that, thought Phoebe. At least Mrs. Ludtz was back to her usual restrained appearance with a tight bun, no makeup and serviceable shoes.

The woman gave her a scowl over her glasses as

Phoebe tossed her shoulder bag on the floor and plopped down into a chair. She started to reach for some old-fashioned looking strawberry wrapped hard candies in a glass bowl on the desk, but a disapproving glare from Mrs. Ludtz had her pulling back her hand.

Phoebe had a definite feeling the woman didn't approve of her. It looked like Amber was right. The woman clearly didn't like other women who dressed fashionably, and with Phoebe's penchant for high heels and bright red lipstick, she was definitely on that list. Today she was dressed more for a heist than a classroom. She had worn black form-fitting pants with black knee-high boots and a black V-neck sweater. She was on a mission after all.

"How may I help you, Professor Pringle?"

Phoebe thought she would try the direct approach.

"I was just at a little teachers' party." She stopped as the bitter woman frowned in disapproval. Rushing on, she said, "And I was hearing some strange rumor that the murders could be connected to this crazy old tale of a mad monk! Do you think that could be true?"

Mrs. Ludtz pulled a key from the center drawer of her desk and stood. Taking up a pile of paperwork, she walked through an adjacent door and returned empty-handed. All the while Phoebe watched and waited.

"I would focus on your duties here and not pay attention to idle gossip, Professor Pringle," Mrs. Ludtz said stiffly as she replaced the key.

"But I just feel so bad for those women," needled Phoebe.

Mrs. Ludtz sniffed. "Don't. Neither of them were

proper young ladies. They were lucky it was not a few hundred years earlier. Back then, they would have probably been burned for witchcraft given their loose morals, provocative dress and unmarried state," sneered the woman as she gave Phoebe a knowing look.

Phoebe's eyes widened at that cruel and callous response, not to mention the not-so-subtle reference to her similarity to the victims.

"Was there something else you needed, Professor Pringle?" Mrs. Ludtz asked, her agitation showing.

"Yes, Mrs. Ludtz. Would you perhaps know if there is a local library in town? I looked online but didn't see one listed. I thought perhaps it didn't have a webpage."

Lifting her lips up in distaste, she asked, "Why would you need a local library? There is an exceptional one here at the school."

"Yes, I know. I just find myself fascinated by some of the local…foliage," lied Phoebe, knowing a reference to local lore would remind Mrs. Ludtz of her interest in the Mad Monk tale and probably bring on another lecture about morals and the proper place of women.

"There is one on Oak Street just off Main. Now if there is nothing else, Professor Pringle, my day does consist of duties outside of entertaining your varied questions."

Recovering, Phoebe thought for second. "Yes. Knowing how you guard the traditions here, I just wanted to let you know I saw a few midshipmen out of uniform on the quad." She leaned in close with a conspiratorial gleam in her eye. "And I think they were wearing jeans!"

With a cry of alarm, Mrs. Ludtz sprang to her feet and

ran straight out the door. The woman could certainly hustle when she thought her precious traditions were not being respected!

Phoebe did not waste a moment. Leaning over the desk, she opened the center drawer. Brushing aside a few prescription bottles of pills and a tiny, souvenir dreamcatcher, she located the key. Rushing through the door which she suspected led to the file room, she wasn't disappointed. Placing the key in the slot on the side of the cabinet, she turned it, unlocking all the drawers. Tossing a quick look over her shoulder, she pulled each drawer open till she found one containing student files. Her fingers slipped over the tabs. Locating the files for Drake and Casey, the two midshipmen she had learned were repeatedly disciplined for troubled behavior, she hustled over to the copier in the corner. Casting another glance through the doorway to the receptionist's area to make sure all was still clear, she began to copy the contents of each file without even risking a look at what they contained.

Grabbing the warm stack of papers straight off the copier, she returned to Mrs. Ludtz's desk to grab her shoulder bag and shove them inside. Now that her copies of the files were secured, she returned to the side room to put back the student files and relock the cabinet.

Just as she was turning the key, she heard footsteps and a low, male voice just outside in the hallway. Knowing she would raise suspicion if she were found in the file room or lurking around Mrs. Ludtz's desk without her near, Phoebe crossed the threshold and slipped into Michael's office, pulling the door almost shut so she could hear but not be seen. If she were in luck it would just be someone dropping off something for Mrs. Ludtz. She was certain it wasn't Michael as he was off campus all afternoon according to Amber.

The male voice came closer. They must be standing directly in front of Mrs. Ludtz's desk. It sounded as if they were on the phone.

Phoebe backed away from the door and leaned against a bookshelf. She tried to listen. You never knew what you may learn listening at keyholes!

"It's no problem. We will just reschedule for later this week."

Her hand flew to cover her mouth. Good God, it was Michael!

And she was hiding *in his office*! This was so stupid of her, thought Phoebe. She should have just brazened it out. It would have been far easier to explain her presence in Mrs. Ludtz's area than *in the commander's office*! Damn it.

"In the meantime, I will send you my report on the possible security holes which led to the murder occurring just off campus grounds and the ways I have rectified them," he said as he continued his call. "I am also waiting on a more detailed report of the students once suspected."

There was a long pause.

Then Michael continued, "I'm aware. Yes. Yes. You have nothing to worry about, sir. I will be discreet."

Her heart was beating so fast and loud, Phoebe swore it would give her away. Clenching her fists to her chest, she leaned over and hazarded a glimpse through the thin slit in the doorway.

Michael was standing in profile in front of Mrs.

Ludtz's desk on his cell. Looking sexy as hell in his dress blues, damn him. And damn the effect all men in uniform had on women, thought an agitated Phoebe.

She watched as he ended the call then leaned over to write a Post-it note which he left in the center of Mrs. Ludtz's desk calendar. He then bent to pick something up.

It was her shoulder bag.

Phoebe thought she might faint as all the oxygen left her lungs. Michael's brow wrinkled as, holding the shoulder bag, he scanned the empty receptionist area.

There wasn't a doubt in Phoebe's mind that the observant Marine recognized it as hers.

Please don't look inside. Please don't look inside. Please don't look inside, chanted Phoebe inside her head.

Getting caught stealing files from the King of Chinatown meant getting screamed at and possibly chased down the street by a man with a carving knife. She didn't even want to think what getting caught by the commander meant.

His intent gaze rested on his partially closed door. Phoebe jerked back, away from the narrow opening, uncertain if he saw her.

She waited, holding her breath.

She heard a rustling of paper and the scrape of a pen. Unable to help herself, she risked another glance through the doorway.

He was writing what looked like another note. He then turned and started to walk out of the office area.

Phoebe closed her eyes in relief. *That was too fucking close*, she thought.

She heard the click of a door. Opening her eyes, she looked again to see if the coast was clear.

Michael had closed one of the double doors. She watched as he adhered the Post-it note to the front. He then closed the second door.

And locked it.

* * *

He could smell her perfume.

It was a sweet floral scent he'd noticed the first day she walked into his office. It suited her. There was no denying he wanted to learn what it smelled like on her soft, warm skin. Then he saw the shoulder bag she seemed never to be without.

She was here, and the little minx was up to something.

Writing a note sending Mrs. Ludtz on some long errand, he closed and locked the doors.

Turning back, he unbuttoned his dress blue coat. He didn't want to be in uniform for what he was about to do. Shrugging out of the coat, he was left in his blue slacks and a silver, Under Armour T-shirt. Thinking he had let her stew long enough, Michael stepped to his office door. Laying a palm flat against its polished surface, he slowly pushed it open. His office looked quiet and undisturbed.

He was not fooled.

He had entered enough enemy encampments to know when a room was occupied.

She was here.

He scanned the room.

Nothing looked disturbed.

He took two steps onto the center of the plush carpet.

There was a slight rush of air as the minx scurried out from her hiding place behind the door and tried to bolt across the threshold to freedom.

She wasn't so lucky.

"Not so fast," he called as his hand flashed out, snatching her back by her slim upper arm.

He pivoted, slamming her back against the wall, wedging her at the end of the bookshelves. Blocking her escape with his own body.

She was breathing heavily but did not say a word. Just stared at him with wild, wide eyes, like a rabbit caught in a predator's snare.

He took his time lowering his gaze over her body, from her red lips to the outline of her breasts in the tight-fitting black sweater to the shape of her hips and legs in her black slacks and leather boots. She was even dressed to be up to no good, he thought with a smile.

Placing a booted foot against her left foot, he kicked it out, spreading her legs open. He stepped forward, fitting his hips against her stomach. Her tiny frame was dwarfed by his powerful one. Sliding his hands down her slender arms, he secured her wrists and wrenched them over her head. He could smell her perfume. The old leather from the books. The faint hint of peppermint on her breath.

"Mind telling me what you are doing breaking into my office, princess?"

Her expressive green eyes flashed at the endearment.

"Don't call me princess," she fired back defiantly.

"Why not? The name fits. A beautiful female who stubbornly runs headlong into danger. That is how fairy tales go, isn't it?" he responded, a wry twist to his lips.

He didn't miss how her eyes focused on his mouth as he talked.

Still, she tried to fight him. "And what? You're my knight in shining armor come to rescue me? To let me go?" she added hopefully.

Securing her wrists in his left hand, he ran the knuckles of his right over her cheek. "Oh, princess. This isn't that type of fairy tale. I'm not that kind of knight. And letting you go is the very last thing on my mind."

His mouth crashed down on hers, finally tasting those cherry red lips. His tongue swept in, teasing her own. He could feel her hips twist as she tried pulling down on her arms. Her tiny sharp teeth sunk into his lower lip. He wrenched his head back. His tongue swept out to taste a small drop of blood. The light of battle shone in her eyes and spurred him on. He could tell she was loving this test of wills as much as he.

Grabbing her jaw with his free hand, he warned her, "Bite me again and I will tear off your clothes here and now and fuck you senseless against the wall."

Testing his resolve, she spat out, "I fucking dare you to try!"

His mouth silenced any further protest. Releasing her arms, his large hands slid over her thighs, pulling them up to straddle his hips. Rubbing his thick shaft between her legs, he tasted her moan. His left hand reached under her turtleneck to seek her warm flesh. He could feel the soft scrape of her lace bra against the center of his palm as he cupped her breast. Using his thumb and forefinger, he ruthlessly pinched her nipple through the thin lace. Phoebe cried out as her hands wrapped around his neck, pulling him closer.

"That's it, baby. Let me hear those cries and moans."

Books and long-forgotten awards fell from the shelves as he rocked into her. Pulsing his hips against her mons, he desperately wanted to sink his hard cock deep inside her wet heat.

Knowing it was impossible. It was the middle of the afternoon. In his office. The commanding officer of the academy's office. There were certain lines even he wouldn't cross.

Licking her lower lip, he grabbed the soft fullness of her ass with his right hand and demanded, "Say my name."

"What?" she asked, breathless and confused.

Nipping at her lower lip, he demanded, "I want to hear these lips call out my name," as his hand squeezed her flesh.

With a challenging flash of her gorgeous eyes, she whispered, "Michael."

The simple sound of her saying his name in that deep throaty voice of hers sent a bolt of lust straight through his cock. Ruthlessly, he harnessed the emotion for later.

Tasting the sweet peppermint of her mouth one last time, he shifted to bury his face in the side of her neck, feeling the warmth of her skin, the soft brush of her hair, inhaling the scent of her.

After several calming breaths, he reached up and unhooked her legs from around his hips, letting her slide back down to the floor, holding her by the hips till she had regained her own breath.

Her lips were swollen and bruised. The pale skin around them stained pink from her smeared lipstick. Her usually sleek hair was tangled and knotted about her heart-shaped face. She looked beautiful. Stunning.

He reached into his pocket and pulled out a folded white handkerchief.

Keeping his blue gaze locked on her emerald eyes that were still darkened by desire, he lifted her sweater and placed the folded cloth against her flat stomach. Holding her eyes, he slid it past her waistband. Pushing his fingers under the fabric of her panties, he cupped her cunt.

Phoebe let slip a shocked gasp.

Running the soft cambric fabric over those sweet lips he had yet to see, Michael pulled the handkerchief free. Flipping the fold over the wet mark, he inhaled the musky scent of her arousal.

"A remembrance," he said before slipping the handkerchief back in his pocket.

Phoebe slipped under his arm and ran through the door.

He watched as she snatched up her shoulder bag and reached to unlock the double doors to the outside world.

"Phoebe," he called out.

She didn't turn but stilled.

"Later. You *will* tell me what you were doing sneaking around my office and what you're *really* doing at this school," he ordered. His voice still raw with lust.

Without saying a word, she unlocked the door and fled.

CHAPTER 8

Phoebe raced to her late afternoon class. While the class discussed Macbeth and the deceptive motivations of Lady Macbeth and how that impacted his performance on the battlefield, Phoebe's mind returned to Michael and what had just happened in his office.

Good God!

Raw, tear-your-clothes-off passion like that—it just didn't happen! That was for movies and romance novels. A man doesn't really just grab a woman and kiss her senseless. Not in real life anyway. Except this man did and Phoebe wasn't sure she would ever recover. It was almost jarring to have your body taken over like that...used and revered at the same time. And his kiss. It was the most all-consuming, amazing kiss she had ever experienced. It was like swallowing sunshine. All heat and energy.

She'd nearly expired on the spot. It was so fucked up and wrong but she couldn't deny the naughty thrill that had tingled down her spine as he grabbed her ass and demanded a response from her. It played perfectly into the recurring schoolgirl spanking fantasy she had about him.

She was so fucked.

Her mind was so lost in the memory she didn't even register the bell ringing. Phoebe gave herself a mental shake. She had to focus. She had a job to do. Waiting until the last person filed out, Phoebe pulled the copied pages from her bag. She wasn't sure what she was looking for, but she hoped something would click.

Neither John Drake nor Robert Casey had parents in politics; still, she jotted down the corporate names on the letters of recommendation and their parents' professions just so she could double-check for any connections. Maybe one of them was a big defense contractor with the military. She then looked at the write-ups. Unlike what Amber implied, she didn't see anything that screamed sociopath-in-training. Noticing both students' interest in biology and science classes, she had a pretty good idea what they were actually doing with that dead squirrel. No, neither boy's file seemed to have any red flags.

Mrs. Ludtz, on the other hand...

* * *

IT TOOK ALL her resolve to finish her teaching obligations and not head straight back to her room to start putting together her notes and trying to make sense of her suspicion of Mrs. Ludtz. She needed to organize her notes and talk with Henry. The idea that she might be wrapping up the story and would have to leave immediately gave her a small pang. There would be no more test of wills with Michael. No more passionate encounters. She would go back to her world and he would stay in his. It was for the best. After he learned of her deception, Phoebe doubted he would ever speak to her again anyway.

She was finishing up her notes when Henry called later that evening.

"How are you doing out there in the boondocks, Wilson? Learn anything yet?"

"Plenty. Did you know there is some crazy tradition up here where they burn a monk in effigy every twenty-fifth of October? And that the symbol carved on the women's chests wasn't a pentagram. There is a good chance it's the symbol of a Native American evil spirit called a wendigo, although I have to get to a library to confirm. The internet doesn't have a reliable source."

"No shit? What about the military's involvement? Find any proof of a cover-up?"

"Well…" Phoebe paused, thinking about the warning in blood on her door. She decided to take precautions. "Hold on a sec, Henry."

Minimizing the phone screen, Phoebe brought up her Pandora account as she turned on the mini Bose speaker she always traveled with. The thumping base of Little Big Town's *Tornado* filled the room. She double-checked that the door was locked before returning to her call.

"Okay, I'm back."

"Did you enter a nightclub?" joked Henry.

"Things are getting a little hinky here. I want to make sure I'm not overheard. Oh! And thanks for telling me I resemble both murder victims! That was a fun little fact to discover once I was already trapped here in Buzzards Bay!"

"I gave you the file," said Henry unapologetically. "It's not my fault you didn't look it over till later."

"It's still creepy as fuck," grumbled Phoebe.

She then related what she had learned from the students' files as well as her careful prodding of several professors and staff around campus. She had even approached a midshipman or two about it.

"I think you're right. There's a story there. Not a big splashy one, but it can't hurt your career to please the owner of the paper," said Henry after hearing all her evidence. "What about the new commander. Do you think he's in on it?"

Bonnie Tyler's *I Need a Hero* started to blare over her speaker.

Phoebe's stomach twisted at the thought. Trying to keep her voice neutral so Henry wouldn't suspect her true feelings about Michael, she responded, "He seems straight. He came after the murders, so I don't think he was involved in deliberately keeping the police out of it or in any cover up, although like I said, I think a member of his staff may be. I just can't wrap my head around the idea of straightlaced Mrs. Ludtz carving up a woman and eating her liver!"

"Jesus Christ, Wilson. I remember when this used to be a gentleman's game."

Phoebe smiled. That was Henry's standard comment whenever she got too casually gruesome with the details of an investigation.

"Well, it's either her or the evil ghost of a mad monk committing murder," quipped Phoebe.

"What the fuck is going on in here?"

Phoebe dropped the phone as she turned to see Michael standing in the middle of her room.

"Phoebe? Who's that? What's going on?"

Recovering the phone from the bed covers, Phoebe could hear the concern in Henry's voice. He never called her Phoebe. "I…I…it's fine. I have to go," she responded as her startled eyes remained on Michael.

"Are you sure you're okay?" asked Henry.

"Yes, I'm fine." *For the moment,* thought Phoebe as she hung up.

Phoebe wasn't sure what to focus on first. The sight of Michael standing before her out of uniform in a pair of jeans and a gray hoodie. The fact that he had entered her locked room. That she didn't know how long he had been standing there or what he had heard. Or maybe just the raw anger that was clearly emanating from his powerful form.

Pants!

Focus on putting on pants first, thought Phoebe as she realized with a start that she was standing dumbfounded before him in just a T-shirt and panties.

Grabbing the first thing she could lay her hands on, the pillow from the bed, she held it over her exposed thighs.

"How the hell did you get in my room? The door was locked!"

"I'm the commander," came his clipped, completely inexcusable response.

"Why are you here?"

"We have some unfinished business, princess."

His blue eyes were iced over. The firm set of his jaw and the way his fists were clenched at his sides told her he was going to be immovable on this front. She would need to have an answer for her strange appearance in his office. Trying to buy herself some time, she accused, "A gentleman would retreat from the room or at least turn around until a lady could cover herself."

"I'm no gentleman. I'm a Marine. We only know how to advance."

Phoebe gave a cry of alarm as he took two determined steps toward her. Having nowhere else to run, she dropped the pillow and jumped up on the bed. Holding her hands out defensively, she warned, "You come near me and I'll scream."

Michael's lips split into a wolfish grin. "You are the only one bunked in this corridor. Scream all you want."

He reached out and grabbed her ankles. Pulling her legs up and wide, causing her to fall backward onto the bed. Standing over her, Phoebe watched as he unzipped his hoodie, exposing a desert-tanned chest and flat stomach ridged with muscle. As he shrugged out of the garment, his wide shoulders and thick biceps were exposed. She remembered her initial impression of him as a marble statue come to life.

"Do I need to tie you to the bed or are you going to be a good girl and give me what I want?" he asked huskily.

Phoebe swallowed. Her stomach clenched as she felt a tingling surge between her legs. Damn, the man knew just how to speak to a woman in a way that both infuriated and inflamed her. She didn't know whether to slap him or kiss him. Damn his arrogant ass!

Part of her wanted to see if he really would be bold enough to tie her to the bed. Just as she was about to turn over and play at still being frightened and fighting him, his hand went to the zipper of his jeans and she was transfixed. She watched as he slowly lowered the zipper, opening the flaps with both hands. Exposing the chiseled cut of his abdomen and hips. The faint dark waves of hair just above his cock…and….

Good God!

He fisted his shaft and pulled it free from its denim confines. Confined. That was a good term for the beast he had just unleashed from inside his jeans. His cock was thick and long with a large bulbous head. It was as threatening as its master.

Now Phoebe wasn't playing. She really was frightened. There was no way this was going to work. No way. She was not *that* girl. The sexually experienced kind who could take a beast of a cock like that in stride.

Leaving his jeans clinging to his hips, Michael placed one knee on the bed between her open legs. Phoebe immediately started to scurry back against the headboard. Once more raising a defensive hand, she stuttered, "Wait…I…we…no…this…can't…you!"

"Don't worry, princess. You'll like it when I make it hurt," he growled as he gripped her thighs and pulled her back down onto the bed. Grabbing the hem of her T-shirt, he whipped it over her head before she could make any further protest.

"Beautiful," he murmured before taking one pert nipple into his mouth.

Phoebe groaned and arched her back as he swirled his tongue around the sensitive tip, only lightly scraping with the edge of his teeth. His warm hand caressed her stomach before shifting between her legs to pull on her panties.

In a panic, Phoebe reached for the thin pink fabric. Her slightly fearful eyes clashed with his determined ones. After a brief tug-of-war, he twisted his hand into a fist and tore the silk off her body.

"No more games, princess. I've won the battle and I want my prize."

Phoebe could not deny the truth. From the moment she had laid eyes on this man, he had both angered and fascinated her. She was drawn to his raw display of power and strength. As much as her mind rebelled, there was no denying her body loved how he just took what he wanted. It made her feel desired. A desire beyond reason or the polite niceties and dictates of society. The rules be damned. She wanted to feel overpowered. Taken.

Fucked.

Raising her arms up to grip the edge of the headboard, she opened her legs wider. A silent assent.

There was a low, dark rumble in Michael's chest as he settled his weight on top of her. She could feel the scrape of metal teeth against the sensitive skin of her inner thighs from the zipper on his jeans. He rose up slightly on his knees as he braced one hand by her head, the other brushing a fallen curl back from her face. The head of his cock pushed against her entrance.

Leaning down, he whispered against her lips, "Baby, this is going to hurt. I need inside you right now like I need to breathe, but if you say no, I'll do all in my power to pull back."

It was the nicest thing this stern and implacable Marine had said to her so far.

After a moment's hesitation, she craned her neck up and gave him a gentle kiss on the lips, unable to form the words.

He nipped at her full lower lip. "There will be no turning back. Once I take what's mine, I keep it."

He talked in forevers.

It was insane. It wasn't real. The way he acted. The way he looked at her. It was with such primal possession. As if she were not just some quick conquest or a tumble in the sheets, but a treasure he would hold onto tightly. Her own reflections on his character came back to her. *He was a man of focus, of determination. Who took what he wanted.*

This wasn't a man who needed months or even weeks getting to know a woman to realize she was what he wanted. This wasn't just an idle statement but a warning.

Phoebe raised her hips as she crossed her ankles over his lower back.

Michael pulled his hips back and thrust hard.

* * *

HER CRY ECHOED in his ears. He wasn't sure if it was from pleasure or pain but he couldn't stop. He was a man possessed. An animal. His only focus was the wet heat of her body and the primal surge of feeling the moment he joined his body with hers. His blood pounded through his veins. His vision blurred. Gripping the sheets on either side of her head, he looked down into her wide, emerald eyes and forcefully thrust his flesh inside her own. Her body clenched around his thick shaft like a vise. Wet heat. Her fingernails clawed down his back. The sting of pain only spurred him on. His hips moved, driving his cock into her cunt. He could feel the sweat bead between his shoulder blades. Smell her own musky scent blending with that of her perfume. A need to mark her even more clearly rose in his chest. Lowering his head, he opened his mouth over her soft shoulder. The tip of his tongue swiped at her skin. Tasting her before his teeth sunk deep.

She moaned at the pain before wrapping her legs more tightly around his hips.

His tongue swept across her skin again, feeling for the crescent indentations of his mark.

"Oh God! Oh God!" she breathed against his chest. "Harder," she screamed.

Michael smiled. Damn she was an amazing woman.

Leaning back on his knees, his hands spanned her hips, lifting her higher till her ass was off the bed and the rest of her weight was resting on her shoulder blades.

"You want it harder, princess," he ground out, "ask me nicely like a good girl."

"*Please!* Fuck me harder," she challenged. A fighting fire in her eye.

He drove full force into her tight cunt. He would make sure she felt the bruise from his touch for days. Placing his thumbs between her thighs, he opened her pussy lips, wanting to see his cock as it thrust inside. Wanting to see how her small body stretched around his thick shaft. The pad of his thumb pressed against her clit. A soft touch despite the violence of his thrusts.

Phoebe moaned and bucked her hips against him, her hands fisting in the sheets over her head. He swirled his thumb again, this time putting more pressure.

She bucked again, her body clenching even tighter around his cock.

"That's it, baby, come for me."

Phoebe's arms lowered as her hands covered her breasts. Squeezing and kneading her own flesh. Michael thrust faster at the sight.

As if she were truly under his command, Phoebe screamed her release.

Michael continued to thrust. Relishing in how her body clenched and gripped his cock while she came, he could feel his balls tighten as the pleasurable pressure increased. One final thrust. He threw his head back and let out a roar of completion as he released deep inside her body. Once again marking her as his own.

* * *

MICHAEL LAY on his back in the narrow bed. Phoebe was snuggled up to his side, a slim thigh tossed over his own. Her head on his shoulder as he caressed her hair.

He had never fucked a woman like that before. It had been almost violent. The fierce need to be inside of her, to mark her, to possess her, had overcome him like a force of nature. Their short acquaintance did not bother him.

Marines learned to not fear the possibility of death tomorrow by living for today. He was drawn to this woman, it was as simple as that. He was drawn to her intelligence, her stubbornness, her spirit. When she'd walked into his office he'd desired her. When he'd seen her standing on that chair reciting Shakespeare as if she were a general trying to inspire her troops into battle, he half fell in love with her. Then later, when she broke into his office and he realized his stubborn princess may be in some kind of danger and every instinct to fight and protect came to the fore, he knew he was in trouble.

Kissing the top of her head, he said, "You need to tell me what is going on. What you are involved in."

He could feel her small frame stiffen. Her gentle breathing stopped.

"I don't know what you mean."

She was lying to him.

"You're being careless and I'm a dangerous man to cross. Something is going on and I need you to tell me what it is so I can handle it for you."

She leaned up on her elbow. Her hair fell in soft waves over her shoulder to tickle his chest. He couldn't see the color of her eyes in the fading light. Despite their dark depths, he knew she was lying.

"I can't and I don't need you to handle anything for me. I can take care of myself."

He brushed the hair off her shoulder. With his fingertip, he traced the fading crimson crescent moons. His mark was already disappearing off her skin.

"'Who knows what intimacies our eyes may shout.

What evident secrets daily foreheads flaunt. What panes of glass conceal our beating hearts?'"

"More poetry." Her tone was low and remorseful.

Michael shrugged his shoulders. "A career in the military can bring a lot of darkness and solitude. I've always turned to books and poetry for companionship and to keep a sense of beauty with me even when surrounded by ugliness."

He watched as her eyes teared up.

"Excuse me," she sniffled as she ran into the bathroom.

Michael rose and lithely crossed the room to her desk. If she wasn't going to trust him with her secrets, he was just going to have to learn them himself. He would be damned if he stood idly by while she could be putting herself in danger. Flipping open the notebook on the desk, he read the careful outline she had written. He was back lounging in bed before she returned.

So his lying little princess was getting herself caught up in the murders. He would just see about that.

Holding out a hand to her, he said, "Come back to bed, babygirl. We'll worry about all this tomorrow."

She gave him a soft smile and curled up again by his side. He could feel her body relax in sleep a few minutes later.

He stayed awake. Watching over her. His sweet, stubborn babygirl.

Planning.

* * *

When Phoebe woke the next morning, he was already gone. Placing a hand on the pillow where he'd slept, she thought back to the poem he'd quoted. It was *Betrayal* by Emily Dickinson. She laid her cheek on the pillow, inhaling the spicy sandalwood of his cologne.

What had she done?

In the span of a heartbeat she was quite possibly falling in love with an arrogant, overbearing, poetry-reciting, passionate, amazing man.

And he would hate her forever when he found out she had been lying to him from the beginning.

CHAPTER 9

Michael tried to control his anger.

It wasn't her lies. It was that she didn't trust him with the truth. It cut him to the core to read in her notes about the symbol painted in blood on her door. That, mixed with what he'd overheard of her conversation, her theft of the student files from his office and what he'd seen in her notebook, convinced him she was putting herself in danger by investigating these murders on her own. But why? And why hadn't she reached out to him when she first was threatened?

He should be fair about this. Not everyone was trained to assess situations as well as character from a first meeting. Not everyone had their instincts honed from years of battle. He shouldn't blame her for not knowing he could be trusted based on their brief acquaintance. It wasn't fair of him to expect it of her.

Problem was, he wasn't in a fair mood.

He was in a vengeful one.

And he wanted answers.

***

"Well, this certainly is a surprise, Colonel. I'm sorry for not getting up to the school myself to greet you properly. We've just been a bit short-handed as of late."

Michael waved away Sheriff Stevens' apologies. "No need, Sheriff. We're both busy men, which is why I would like to get straight to the point."

The sheriff was a tall, lanky man of about sixty. With his large, white handlebar mustache, he gave the impression of belonging more in an old western frontier town than a small bay village in Massachusetts. With a nod of understanding, he motioned for Michael to join him in his office. "Dolores, don't bug me," called out the sheriff before shutting the door. Michael smiled, liking the man instantly.

Sheriff Stevens placed two coffee mugs on his desk. Opening the bottom drawer, he pulled out a bottle of bourbon. "It ain't morning drinking if it's medicinal," he said with a sly wink before pouring them both a generous amount.

After taking a swallow, the sheriff leaned back in his chair. "I expect you are here to ask me about those poor women."

"If you forgive me for saying so, Sheriff, there wasn't much of an investigation by your department."

Stevens gave him a rueful smile. "You don't get to be sheriff of this area for going on twenty years by interfering with the Puller Academy's business, son."

"Still, I'm sure you have your opinions."

Stevens gave Michael an assessing look, then took

another swallow of bourbon. "You're not their typical superintendent. Usually I'm sitting across from an old salt admiral who just wants a soft assignment to ride out till retirement."

"The military will always be needed, but in order to stay relevant to truly fulfill its purpose to society, it needs to accept new ideas and be open to new perspectives. That starts, I believe, with the officers and how they are educated before taking on their first post. I realized early in my military career that my education at Puller was one of the most impactful as far as shaping me as a leader. After my last tour, I decided it was the best possible way for me to do my part."

The sheriff nodded his head. After a long, thoughtful pause, he said, "We were first on the scene. The murders happened just off campus so the academy wasn't involved at that point. I'm sure you've seen the official report."

Michael nodded his head. "Stripped and strangled. No sign of sexual assault. Liver missing. Carving of a satanic symbol. I know once the academy got involved, the police were pulled out. I will tell you there was an extensive investigation done, at least when it came to a possible midshipman's involvement. There were two suspected students initially, but it proved to be nothing. I'll be frank with you, that is all my report contains on the subject. That and instructions to increase security around campus."

The sheriff shook his head and leaned back in his chair. He poured himself another finger of bourbon before continuing. "There was something not right about that whole scene. You know, besides the gruesome Satan shit."

"In what way?"

"In the autopsy, it mentioned post-mortem scratches on their backs. Seems to me that meant they were dragged onto the rock. Because the women were naked, everyone assumed it was a man who'd done it. These were two slight women. Seems to me a man wouldn't have to drag them onto the rock. Just place 'em there."

But a woman would, thought Michael, recalling Phoebe's notes on Mrs. Ludtz being a possible suspect. This was a small town. Michael wasn't sure if the sheriff knew or would be loyal to Mrs. Ludtz, and he didn't want to ruin the woman's reputation with a false accusation, especially with something as serious as murder.

"Were there any female suspects?" he asked instead.

The sheriff shook his head. "Nah. Never got that far. Navy swept in and took over. Claimed it was close enough to the academy that they wanted jurisdiction. Like I said, no point in getting in a pissing match over it, especially when I don't have the staff or resources to investigate two murders."

Sounded about right, no one wanted a scandal. It was better to blame a faceless drifter and play the odds that it was an isolated incident.

Michael rose and extended his hand. "Thank you, Sheriff. You've been helpful."

Shaking his hand, the sheriff added, "I can't see how the academy or the Navy would appreciate you poking around in this, son. You're going to make some people awful angry."

"Well, at least these angry people won't be trying to kill me with a homemade pipe bomb or Soviet-era gun, so I consider it an improvement over my last assignment."

He left the sheriff's office with another target in mind. It was past time he confronted his little lying princess.

Michael turned up the collar of his wool overcoat and grabbed the rim of his cover as he walked away from his car. The wind off the bay had picked up. Looking to the sky, he saw fierce black rainclouds gathering. It was going to be one hell of a storm. Holding the flaps of his collar closed, he made his way back to the main building. The dark chaos of the weather matched his mood.

All he cared about was finding Phoebe and getting some fucking answers. That was when he saw his quarry.

She was headed toward the school library.

CHAPTER 10

Leaving the main floor of the library behind, Phoebe headed to the back corner and climbed the two flights up the small brass spiral staircase to the upper level loft. With the books on math, science and military history on the lower levels, this part of the library containing books on local history, poetry and art did not see as much traffic. Since it was also the dinner hour, the majority of the midshipmen would be in the mess hall. Phoebe tossed her shoulder bag onto the worn window seat of the large bay window which overlooked Buzzards Bay and created a cozy nook between the stacks and began her search. She was hoping to find a few volumes on the Wampanoag and their shaman beliefs. Phoebe wanted to know if there was more than one way to kill a wendigo, perhaps by strangling.

Phoebe was so absorbed in her search, she didn't hear his approach.

"Taking a sudden interest in local lore, babygirl?"

She turned with a start. Michael filled the tiny space

between the book stacks. His wide shoulders practically touching each shelf. She couldn't help but notice how handsome he looked in his blue uniform. So authoritative. So…male. The recurring unwanted thought brought a familiar tingling reaction.

"As a matter of fact, yes." Phoebe placed the book she was reviewing back on the shelf as nonchalantly as possible. Although there was nothing suspicious about reading a local history book, she had this instinctive feeling that Michael would find it so.

He took a step toward her.

In a panic, Phoebe turned her back on him. Facing the stacks, she nervously fingered the bindings of the books as she tried to calm her erratic breathing. The air was filled with the scent of his cologne and old leather from the books. She felt rather than heard him take another step closer. His hand appeared slightly above her head to the left as he gripped the hard wooden edge of the bookshelf. It seemed large and masculine with just the faintest crisscross pattern of white scars across the knuckles. A souvenir from past fights. Fights he'd probably won.

With the alcove to her right and his large form blocking her exit to the left, she was trapped. Caged between his body and the bookshelf.

There was the brush of his hand along the pleats of her skirt. She was wearing a purple pleated skirt with her knee-high black boots and a gray V-neck sweater. As she felt the soft fabric brush the back of her thigh, she became painfully aware of the fact she wasn't wearing any stockings. His hand brushed the skirt again. This time the tips of his warm fingers played with the hem, skimming her thigh.

"You're lying," he said gruffly just over her shoulder as the knuckles of his right hand brushed the curve of her ass. "Bad girls who lie get their asses spanked."

Her heart skipped a beat. Still, she needed to brazen this out. He couldn't possibly have found out she was a journalist…could he?

"No, I'm not. I'm here in the local history stacks," she anxiously whispered as she tried to shift away from his taunting touch.

Phoebe could feel a tremor rock his body right before he grabbed her shoulder and twisted her around, slamming her back against the books. Placing his right hand on the shelf by her head, he had her well and truly cornered. Even in the dimmed lighting between the stacks she could see the bright light of anger in his eyes. He wasn't just resting his hands on the shelves, he was *gripping* them. His whole body radiated rage.

"You're lying to me," he said through clenched teeth.

"I—"

"No. Don't you fucking dare deny it. I know about the blood on your door. The warning. How could you not come to me?"

"I—"

"I don't know why you are investigating these murders, but I can tell you this. It stops right here…right fucking now."

"You can't order me to stop!" she fired back.

"The hell I can't. I am your commander and you will *not* defy me in this."

"You're not *my* commander and nothing you say is going to stop me from finding out the truth about what happened."

His head reared back as he sucked in a long breath through his nose. The heat of his anger was palpable. She could feel the hard ridge of his cock as it pressed against her stomach. It was a threat, a promise.

"Not your commander?"

She could feel the rumble in his chest as he practically growled the words.

Phoebe hesitantly shook her head no. Her stomach clenched as she tightened her inner thighs, mashing them together. God help her but this clash of wills turned her on. There was a sick thrill in courting danger, and there was no mistaking that defying Michael was courting danger.

"You're right. I'm not your commander. I'm your man and it's about time you recognize my authority and accept my protection."

Before she could protest, his head swooped down, attacking her mouth, claiming her for his own. He tasted like whiskey and coffee. Warm hands ran up the sides of her thighs to grip her ass. Phoebe's eyes sprang open when she felt the tips of his fingers tease the seam between her bottom cheeks before they slid between her clenched thighs to caress her through the thin fabric of her panties.

"You're already wet. For me," he said against her mouth, nipping at her bottom lip while two fingers played with the seam of her panties before dipping underneath to feel the soft lips of her pussy.

"Oh God," moaned Phoebe as she clutched at his shoulders. The harsh feel of the damp wool of his overcoat strangely snapped her out of a heated seductive haze. "Wait! Stop! You can't! Someone will see."

"I don't give a damn, princess."

Easily lifting her against his strong frame, Michael stepped to the side and sat on the bay window bench, forcing her to straddle his hips. The soft lining of his thick overcoat cushioned her knees and Phoebe couldn't focus. It was as if she were floating under a sea of warm water.

Michael's hands dipped into the V-neck of her sweater and ruthlessly forced it down, exposing the soft curves of her breasts. Keeping his intense gaze trained on her, he slowly lowered his head. She watched as the tip of his tongue flicked her pert nipple. Her head fell back, a moan escaping her lips as her eyes squeezed shut.

"Look at me, baby," he ordered.

She obeyed.

Once again riveted by his gaze, she was transfixed as his tongue swirled around her nipple. Teasing her.

Phoebe rocked her hips, rubbing herself on his cock through the heavy fabric of his uniform pants, feeling a thrill of victory when he moaned in response.

His arms wrapped around her middle and yanked her closer as his mouth descended on her breast, sucking the nipple in deep, allowing his teeth to skim her flesh as he laved her with his tongue.

Phoebe's fingers gripped his hair as she pulled him closer. The metal buttons and medal ribbons on his uniform coat scratched her delicate flesh. The slight twinges of pain and the cold, harsh feel of metal against her warm skin only spurred her on.

"Goddammit, woman. I need to fuck you," he ground out as he wedged his hand between their entwined bodies. Lifting her skirt up in front, he fisted the sheer fabric of her thong and pulled, snapping the tiny piece of material in two.

Over their harsh breathing she could hear him unbuckle his belt. Tilting her hips upward, she rubbed herself against the back of his hand as he lowered his zipper, freeing his thick shaft.

"Lift up on your knees."

Phoebe hesitated. As with the last time, she felt a pang of fear over the idea of taking his large cock into her body, knowing it would give equal measures of pleasure and pain.

"Lift up on your knees," he repeated, his voice harsh with lust. "If I have to ask again, I will flip you over and fuck you from behind."

"I don't—" breathed Phoebe, overwhelmed by his arrogant possession of her body.

The wide head of his cock pushed against her tight entrance. There was a sting of pain as he forced it in, but then he paused.

"Just say yes." His demanding tone let Phoebe know he would give no quarter in the matter. "I want to hear you say it."

Phoebe tried to sink her hips down, to push her own body onto his shaft but his large hands on her hips prevented her.

"No. Say it, baby." His eyes glowed a dark, cobalt blue

under lowered brows. His heavy, even breathing mingled with her own.

Running both her hands along the harsh planes of his jaw, feeling the scratch from his five o'clock shadow against her palms, Phoebe captured his gaze.

"Yes, Michael."

With a guttural groan, Michael pushed down on her hips, impaling her small body on his cock. Her cry of painful pleasure was swallowed by his kiss. He started to move. Driving his hips upward, he thrust inside of her. Phoebe's body was thrown against his chest from the force of his thrusts. Reaching past his shoulders, she laid her palms flat against the cold windowpanes.

The threatening black clouds had finally broken into a fierce storm. Heavy raindrops splattered against the glass as the wind outside raged and howled.

The tumult outside matched the one inside the library.

Grabbing her hip with one hand and covering her mouth with the other, he began to pound into her small body. His hips lifted off the bench with every thrust as she rode his cock.

"Come for me, baby," he rasped along the column of her neck as he sunk his teeth into her skin.

The windows behind him had begun to cloud over with condensation from the heat of their bodies. She could hear the hum and bustle of people on the floors below them. Yet nothing else mattered but the strong feel of his arms wrapped around her middle and the pulsing thrust of his cock between her legs. Feeling her body tighten as the pressure built, Phoebe leaned back, trusting in his grasp. Her upper body felt suspended in mid-air.

Tightening her knees against his hips, his cock went in even deeper. Opening her mouth on a silent scream, her eyes screwed shut as she threw her head back, relishing in the waves of dizzying pleasure which crashed over her.

She was only dimly aware of his muted groan as he came deep within her tight passage. His large hand splayed over the soft skin of her stomach as they both waited for the final tremors, the pulsing pleasure, to ebb.

* * *

PHOEBE FELT shy and anxious as they descended the small brass spiral staircase. Michael insisted on carrying her stack of books. Searching the faces of the few midshipmen hanging about the lower level as well as the older man who was checking out her books, Phoebe was relieved to see no censure. Tucked away in the quiet upper loft, no one seemed to have suspected what she and the commander had been about.

Exiting the library, the frigid blast of air tinged with stinging raindrops cooled her heated cheeks.

"I...well...um...I guess I'll be going now," she said awkwardly as she tried to shove the books on local Indian tribes into her shoulder bag.

His only response was a low chuckle. "Where is your coat?"

"I don't have one with me. It's fine. It's only a short walk to my building."

Ignoring her protests, he shook off his wool overcoat and placed it over her shoulders. She was instantly enveloped in the warmth of his scent. Then taking her shoulder bag from her, he placed an arm around her lower back and guided them past the archway onto the rain-slicked path back to her building.

Neither said a word as she pulled open the heavy metal door to her building. She shrugged out of his coat and started to say thank you, hoping to leave him at the entrance.

Michael grabbed her hand and led the way down the hall.

Once at her door, Phoebe tried again to hand him his coat and get him to leave. She needed time to process what had just happened.

The passion. His anger. His accusation. *The spanking kink fantasy.*

It was all swirling about her head.

After another awkward attempt, Michael grabbed her by the chin and forced her gaze to his. "I'm not leaving, princess."

With a sigh, Phoebe rummaged through her shoulder bag till she found her room key. As she pushed it into the lock, she realized the door was already open. Pushing it wide, she flicked on the light and let out an exclamation. Before she could utter a word, Michael's arm swept in front of her, immediately placing her body protectively behind his own.

"Step back. Stay in the hall," Michael ordered as he took a step into her room. He maneuvered quickly around the confined space. Checking the closet, bathroom and under the bed.

Phoebe took a tentative step into her room.

Her trashed room.

The bed covers were ripped to shreds and the mattress tossed. Clothes were scattered about the room. The desk and chair were on their sides. On the wall over her bed, in blood, was the symbol of the wendigo, a large circle with several crisscrossing lines and the overlapping drawing of a skeletal face in the center.

She watched in shocked silence as Michael pulled her suitcase from the closet and began picking up her strewn clothes and tossing them in.

"What are you doing?" she asked.

"You're not staying here. Grab your things from the bathroom. You're coming with me."

Rubbing her face, trying to quell the rising fear in her chest, Phoebe struggled to stay calm and focused. "It's fine. I can pack my own things. I'll grab a room at the motel in town."

Circling around the bed, Michael stormed toward her. Grabbing her by the shoulders, he said, "Do you honestly think I'm going to allow you to stay in a motel?"

"This is not about what you will or will not *allow*! You can't just order me about! You don't own me!" she raged. It wasn't really anger at him or even his high-handed protectiveness. She was frightened and lashing out. This was supposed to be just some quick story she did to please the owner of the paper. Now her life was being threatened by some crazy person who probably thought they were possessed by the fucking Mad Monk's ghost! What the fuck!

"The minute you walked through my office door you became mine, which means you're mine to protect. I don't care if I have to toss you over my shoulder and drag you back to my place kicking and screaming, but rest assured, babygirl, you are spending the night with me…in my bed…under my protection. You got that?"

Faced with well over six feet of dominant male determination, Phoebe could only nod yes.

CHAPTER 11

With no further protest from Phoebe, Michael gathered all her things and ushered her out the door. The commander of the academy was afforded a small brick home on the edge of campus. With neither of them having an umbrella, there was nothing left to do but run through the sheets of rain till he reached his front door. Leading her inside, he began to turn on the lights. Sparing a glance for Phoebe, he was alarmed by how small and vulnerable she looked. Walking over to her, he easily swept her into his arms and carried her upstairs. Placing her on the bed, he went into the master bathroom and began to run a hot bath. All the while, she sat there still and silent.

Michael walked up to her. "Arms up."

She obeyed without a fight…which worried him.

He carefully pulled her gray sweater over her head. He then unlatched her black lace bra. Tossing them both on the bed, he knelt before her and removed first one then the other knee-high boot, giving each chilled foot a comforting squeeze. Lifting her under the arms, he raised her to her feet and unhooked her skirt, letting it fall to the floor. He had what was left of her black thong still tucked in his pocket from their lovemaking in the library. Picking her up once again, he carried her into the bathroom and slowly lowered her into the steaming hot water. The impact of the water thawed her reserve.

Phoebe grabbed onto his upper arm.

"There's something I need to tell you. I'm not a—"

Michael stopped her with a finger to her lips. "It can wait. You take a nice hot bath while I prepare dinner for us. We'll talk then."

Leaving her to soak in the tub, Michael walked back into the bedroom and stripped out of his wet uniform. Tossing on only a pair of jeans, he walked barefoot downstairs. Checking that the front door was locked, he headed to the hall closet. Pressing his thumb to the fingerprint lock on the safe inside it, he removed his 9mm Glock the moment the door sprung open. Grabbing a loaded magazine, he closed the safe door and headed into the kitchen. With the gun within reach, he began to prepare dinner for them both.

* * *

PHOEBE ARRIVED downstairs dressed only in one of his white dress shirts and a pair of his white tube socks. The socks were so large they looked like leg warmers over her small calves. His shirt reached to well below mid-thigh. Michael felt his gut clench. It was the first time he was seeing her without her standard cat-eye makeup and red lips. She looked beautiful.

"I left my suitcase down here, so I borrowed one of your shirts. I hope you don't mind."

"I don't mind in the least," he said with a wink. "Sit. Wine?"

At her nod, he poured them both a glass of cabernet. Heading back into the kitchen, he returned with their plates and joined her at the table.

"I hope you like spaghetti and meatballs. It's the one thing I know how to cook well."

"Actually, it's one of my favorite dishes."

"Good."

They both sat in silence for several minutes. Michael eating. Phoebe mostly twirling the pasta around her fork and taking fortifying sips of wine.

"You know, I'm a pretty sensitive guy. You're going to hurt my feelings if you don't at least pretend to like my cooking," he said teasingly.

Phoebe smiled. "I'm sorry. I guess I'm just not that hungry."

"Grab the bottle and our glasses and head into the living room. I'll join you in a minute."

"No. I'll help with the dishes."

"No you won't and that's an order."

He was pleased when she obeyed him without further argument. After cleaning up, he joined her. The living room was furnished comfortably in masculine shades of royal blue, maroon and gold. Engravings of notable naval ships graced the walls. To warm up the room while she was in her bath, Michael had lit a fire in the beautiful brick fireplace that dominated one wall. As he walked in, he noticed she was curled up on the sofa with one of the throw rugs covering her legs.

He had never been the sort to want to settle down, but seeing Phoebe in his home, wearing his shirt, gave him a strong desire to want to spend every night like this…with her. Sitting next to her on the sofa, he watched and waited. He had learned through years of interrogations of enemy combatants in the military that silence was actually one of the greatest motivators to get someone to talk.

After several minutes, she broke. "How much do you know?"

Stroking his knuckles down her cheek, he said, "Sorry, princess, that's not how this is going to work. You're going to tell me everything. Right here. Right now."

Watching her sigh as she toyed with the stem of her wine glass, he could practically hear her weighing her options. Hopefully, she would come to the correct conclusion.

She had only one. Him.

He knew he wasn't going to like what she had to say. There was no denying she had been lying to him, probably from the start. He just needed to know how much she had been lying about. The one thing he was confident about was she was not lying about her reaction to him. What they had was too raw, too primal to be a lie. He also knew she had placed herself in danger by trying to investigate alone the murders of those two women. What he didn't know was why.

She tucked a lock of honey blonde hair behind her ear

before meeting his eye. Taking a deep breath, she said, "My name isn't Phoebe Pringle."

Michael smiled. "I figured as much, although I have to confess, I like Phoebe. It suits you."

"My name is Phoebe…but it's Wilson. Phoebe Wilson."

"So, Phoebe Wilson, mind telling me what you are doing at my academy and why you lied?"

"I'm an investigative journalist. I'm here to see if there was a naval cover-up of the murders of Mary Bruen and Annie Porter," she burst out in a rush. Her eyes were wide and glistening as she waited for his response.

A journalist.

He figured as much. Her shoes were far too impractical for her to be private investigator. He had warned his supervisors in the Navy it would only be a matter of time before someone from the press caught wind of the story. The details of the murder were too salacious, too gruesome.

"And what have you learned?"

"Wait. You're not going to comment on what I just said?"

"What is there to say?"

Amused, he watched her beautiful green eyes light with anger and defiance.

"Nothing. There is nothing to say," she burst out, obviously hurt.

If he'd doubted for a moment she felt anything for him beyond his usefulness in her investigation, she just chased it away right there with her disgruntled pout. His adorable princess thought he was being dismissive of her…of them. She was mistaking his lack of response, his calm demeanor, for disregard. Mistakenly thinking he regarded her as a quick fuck so her real name didn't matter. It was past time she realized she was his…and he played for keeps.

Taking the wine glass from her fingers, he placed it on the coffee table with his own. He then grabbed her arms and pulled her over his lap.

"What are you doing?" she cried out.

Flipping up the hem of the white shirt, he bared her ass. Raising his arm, he brought his hand down on her right cheek. The loud crack as his palm met her skin echoed around the quiet room.

"Are you crazy?" she screeched.

"That was for lying to me about your name."

He raised his arm again and spanked her left cheek. A cherry red palm print appeared almost immediately. "That was for putting yourself in danger."

Phoebe kicked and screamed but could not dislodge his restraining arm across her lower back.

Deliberately spanking the generous under curve of each bottom cheek, he yelled over her hollering, "And that was for thinking that what we have is so superficial it can't survive a few obstacles. Do I need to continue?"

"No! No! Let me up," she begged.

Flipping her back into an upright position, he could see her cheeks were tinged pink as tears glistened in her eyes.

"I don't think you're allowed to spank an employee like that," she pouted as she crossed her arms over her chest.

"I did anyway," he responded, a challenging light in his eye. "And I will do it again if you ever lie to me again."

Phoebe nodded her understanding.

"Good. Now tell me why you suspect my disagreeable secretary of murder."

* * *

THEY SPENT the next few hours going over everything. They had cleared the kitchen table to make room for the books she had gotten at the library, her copies of the student files, and his copy of the naval and police reports.

"Here, right here. I knew it. It's not a pentagram with a crude carving of Satan. It's the wendigo," exclaimed Phoebe as she held up the dusty old volume they had checked out of the library. It was the published journal of a fur tracker from the seventeenth century. It was a wealth of firsthand information on the tribes in the Buzzards Bay area at the time.

Michael pinched the bridge of his nose. "I'm still not seeing how a three-hundred-and fifty-year-old ghost story somehow plays into a random murder from today."

"That's because you are trying to think through it logically," explained Phoebe.

"Well logical thinking is part of the Marine training," quipped Michael.

Her eyes narrowed in a glare. He loved pushing her buttons. Damn, he couldn't ever remember having this much fun with a woman, despite the fact that the topic of conversation was two gruesome murders.

"We agree that the murders could not have been done by the two suspected midshipmen, right?"

He nodded. "Right. They don't fit the profile and they both have alibis for the time period of both murders."

"I've also determined that neither has any particularly influential parent which would have led us to suspect meddling with the details of their alibis or any other such nonsense."

"We both agree the homeless man theory is just bullshit put out by the Navy."

"I'm surprised you would admit to that."

Michael shrugged. "Marine."

Phoebe laughed. "Is that your answer for everything?"

"Yes," he responded, giving no quarter.

He watched as her expression grew thoughtful. "Is that also why you are handling the news of my being a journalist investigating a possible cover-up in stride? Because it impacts the Navy and perhaps not you as a Marine?"

"No. I'm handling this in stride because we both want the same thing. The truth. I became a Marine to protect the vulnerable. I have absolutely no interest in letting a murderer go free because it might cause the Navy some momentary bad press."

"Collaborating with me could cost you your job," she whispered. "You have to know that is not what I want out of this."

Michael stroked her cheek. "Babygirl, I wouldn't have been assigned this position if my superiors thought I would just look the other way. I was brought here to change the old boy way of thinking. Trust me. They are perfectly aware of my character and what I am capable of.

My career will be just fine. And besides, if you think any of this compares with what I had to deal with in Fallujah—" He left the rest unsaid.

He liked how she blushed at his words and touch. Yeah, he could definitely get used to having her around. She was a fascinating mix of intelligence and vivacity coupled with stubbornness and just the right amount of crazy.

Clearing her throat, she continued. "I know it is a stretch but hear me out. Mrs. Ludtz went off the deep end two months ago after her husband was found cheating on her. I've heard stories of all sorts of erratic behavior."

Phoebe then related to him the strange scene she'd witnessed the day of his run. How Ludtz had been dancing and singing strange nursery rhymes in the woods. It was odd, to be certain, but that didn't make her a murderer.

"Yes, but how does being pissed at a piece of shit husband suddenly lead to murder?"

"That's the piece of the puzzle I don't have," she admitted. "I agree with your sheriff and the police report about the markings on the women's backs, that it could be an indication of a woman unable to lift the dead weight. It would also explain why the victims were strangled and not burned. I can't say I know for certain, but I imagine there is a great deal more involved with trying to burn a body than simply strangling someone. The fact that it perhaps requires more strength and agility than Mrs. Ludtz possesses could be another argument for it being a woman who committed the murders. Plus, people would have seen the fire and come running, possibly catching her in the act."

"And how does the whole mad monk and wendigo tradition fit in?"

"At first I thought it was just some nonsense, but now I'm not so sure. It says here the wendigo was not just associated with cannibalism but also insatiable greed, gluttony and selfishness. What if Mrs. Ludtz has truly come unhinged and she associated those women with the woman who stole her husband away, that she somehow equated his mistress with selfishness and greed for taking something that wasn't hers?"

"Do you think it's possible Mary Bruen was Mr. Ludtz's mistress?"

"It's possible. What if Mrs. Ludtz believes that after killing Bruen she herself became a wendigo? There was the bit about the liver missing. What if Mrs. Ludtz…ate it? Cannibalism leads to a human transforming into the evil spirit of a wendigo," mused Phoebe out loud.

"You realize how insane all this sounds?"

"I do," she admitted.

"Right, well tomorrow after you leave I will track down Mrs. Ludtz's husband. If anyone would have answers for us, it would be him," said Michael as he gathered their empty wine glasses and the empty bottle and took them into the kitchen.

Phoebe followed behind. "I'm sorry. Did you just say *after I leave?*"

"Yes."

She folded her arms across her chest. "I'm not going

anywhere. This is my story and my investigation. I'm going to see it through."

Michael grabbed her by the waist and lifted her high till she was sitting on the counter. With the raised height, she was at eye level with him. Placing a hand on either side of her hips, he leaned in close. "Listen very carefully, princess. You are catching the first flight out of here tomorrow. Just because I didn't mention the fact that you are the fucking spitting image of the two victims doesn't mean I didn't notice. I clocked that the moment I laid eyes on you that first day in my office. Why do you think I tried to get you to leave?"

"So? Lots of woman look like me!"

Grabbing her by the back of the neck, he pulled her in for a quick kiss. "No, beautiful, they don't. You are obviously her next target. She has made that more than clear with the symbol on your door and the ransacking of your room. If it is her, she is becoming even more erratic and unpredictable. Who knows what she will do next? Unfortunately, I can't have her arrested without more proof. I'll talk to her future ex-husband and hopefully learn enough for the sheriff to get an arrest or search warrant. In the meantime, I want you somewhere safe…far away from here."

Phoebe opened her mouth to object.

"Don't argue with me on this, Phoebe. My mind is made up. When this is all over, I'll come and get you."

He should have been suspicious the moment she grew silent. The moment she didn't fight him. Instead, his mind was on more pleasurable pursuits.

* * *

After a brief truce where they spent an amazingly passionate night in bed and enjoying the feel of her in his arms when he awoke, the peace between them was once more broken when she broached the subject of her leaving.

"I'm not," Phoebe insisted.

"Trust me. You are," he fired back.

They continued to argue, kiss, make love, then return to arguing all morning till the late afternoon. Then the time came for her to get into a taxi to the airport and for him to leave for his meeting with Mr. Ludtz.

Wrapping his arm around her lower back, he pulled her close. Placing a hand under her chin, he lifted her face to his. "This isn't over between us. Once it is safe, I will come to New York for you."

He wasn't sure what would happen after that, if she would consider staying with him in Massachusetts or if he would need to find an assignment in New York, but it honestly didn't matter to him.

He had found something he wanted.

Her.

And he would do whatever it took to keep her safe and by his side.

Tapping her on the nose, he teased, "And don't worry. I promise to share all the gory details with you for your story. You will get no military cover-up from me. If you are right about Ludtz, then it is you who solved this case, and you earned the right to write about it."

Phoebe nodded and got into the taxi without another word.

Again, he should have been suspicious. He should have questioned her uncharacteristic silence. Her lack of fight.

He should have known she would defy him.

CHAPTER 12

Present day, later that evening.
Hush now, Phoebe, do not you fear
Never mind, Phoebe, the Mad Monk is near

The sickly-sweet sing-song voice echoed around her empty bedchamber. Phoebe's mouth opened, the lower lip trembling in a macabre pantomime of a silent scream. Fear kept her immobile. A fear so intense it struck straight through her, making her very bones feel brittle and weak. A cold sweat broke out over her brow as she searched the darkness in vain, trying to peer past the moving shadows. Every outline was suspect. Every hint of sound, real or imagined, a cry of alarm, but there was nothing.

Through the distorted glass of her window, she could see the burnt orange and crimson glow from the macabre dance of flickering flames as black-cloaked figures ran about with torches.

Casting a glance to her left, she could see a faint halo of light surrounding the cracks at the edges of the door.

Through it was the dark outline of a heavy bolt. The door was locked tight. Of course, someone had managed to get into her locked room before this.

It had been a warning.

A warning to stay away, to leave this place.

A warning she was putting herself in danger.

A warning she had ignored.

It was a small, single-room chamber with just enough space for a bed, desk and cozy chair in the corner. Barely larger than a student's dorm room. Surely she would know if someone had entered the chamber.

Leaning over, she flicked the switch to the dome ceiling light. Phoebe both craved the security the brightness would bring and dreaded what it might show.

Nothing happened.

Darkness still reigned.

She felt a fresh wave of terror. It took Phoebe a moment to recall she had removed the light bulb herself earlier in case *he* had tried to search her room looking for her. She'd wanted the darkness to shield her, to hide her from his prying, intense gaze but now she wondered what else the darkness was hiding. Had someone else learned of her true purpose for being there? Learned about the lies she'd told to get to the truth?

Again she scanned the darkness. The chamber was silent and still save for the distant shouts and cries from those outside.

Maybe she was just imagining it?

Her nerves were already strung tight from hiding from *him*…from *lying* to him. It only made sense her imagination would lean toward the dark and forboding, that her mind would conjure up monsters under the bed and a mad monk specter to go bump in the night.

Hush now, Phoebe, do not you fear
Never mind, Phoebe, the Mad Monk is near

The raspy voice was definitely coming from inside her bedchamber.

Phoebe launched herself at the door. Throwing the bolt, she ran into the hallway. She was halfway down the long corridor before the chill of the flagstone seeped through her thin socks. In her haste, she had not even grabbed her boots. Throwing a nervous look over her shoulder, she saw the corridor remained empty. The darkness was broken by shafts of weak, blood-stained light. Its source a row of tall, cathedral windows along one wall. Each window had a ruby red cross of Saint John in its center, a remnant from the school's monastic past. A luminous full moon shown through each cross, bathing the space in an eerie red glow. Keeping an eye on the empty corridor, Phoebe reached into her back pocket for her phone. Needing a sense of safety no matter how meager, she leaned against the cold stone wall, protecting her back. She pressed the power button and waited for the screen to come to life.

No bars.

The earlier storm must have knocked out what passed for cell service in this remote area. Phoebe didn't even know who she would call. The police? Would they even dare to cross through the gates onto the property? Probably not. Worse, they would probably just call *him* and expect him to handle the situation. At that very moment, she wasn't certain what she was more afraid of…the possible murderer haunting her...or *his* wrath when he found out she had disobeyed him.

One thing was for certain, she needed to keep moving. Needed to find someplace to hide. Someplace no one would think to look for her.

For a brief moment, she wondered if she dared to return to her chamber for her boots but then thought better of it. She would go to the gymnasium. The locker room would be a bright open space and perhaps she could borrow a pair of shoes from one of the open lockers.

With at least an immediate plan in place, Phoebe headed off down the corridor, feeling more confident the further away she got from the twisted rhyme and whoever was singing it. Stopping before a somber-looking portrait of some old man in a white wig who seemed to be staring down at her in disapproval, Phoebe tried to remember where the gym was in the labyrinth of old hallways and buildings.

The moment's distraction cost her dearly.

A strong arm wrapped around her middle as a large hand covered her mouth, stifling any hope of a scream for help. The hard, unrelenting form pressed along her back radiated masculine strength. Phoebe kicked out as her nails clawed at the hand covering her lips. Desperate to escape, she tried twisting and turning her body. The band of muscle wrapped tightly across her stomach squeezed harder, pressing painfully into her ribs, cutting off her air. Wrenching her head to one side, Phoebe tried to break his grasp. Her stockinged toes scraped along the flagstone for purchase as, with his superior strength, he easily lifted her off her feet.

Still she fought.

Then she heard a deep, throaty chuckle.

Warm lips skimmed the shell of her left ear. She could feel the faint touch of his breath along the exposed delicate skin of her neck. Inhaling precious air through her nose, she caught the spicy scent of his cologne.

"I warned you what would happen if you defied me, princess."

Phoebe's bright green eyes grew wide at the darkly whispered threat cloaked in an endearment. Her pleas were muffled nonsense from beneath his hand.

Already lightheaded from her fevered gasps for breath, she failed to fight when he shifted his grasp to effortlessly lift her over one powerful shoulder.

"You need to learn that no one… no one… defies my command."

She could feel him pivot. Just as he crossed a threshold and slammed the door shut behind them, she reclaimed her voice.

The faint echo of her cry was swallowed by the dark shadows of the cold, uncaring stone corridor.

* * *

"Let me go!" she raged as she pounded on his lower back.

Michael had flung her over his shoulder and carried her down another long corridor and then into a darkened room. As he flicked the light switch, she saw the familiar chairs and desks of her own classroom. Striding to the front, he finally dropped her back onto her feet.

Pushing her hair back, she stormed, "What the fuck, Michael?"

Getting right down in her face, he paused a hairsbreadth away from her. Raising both his hands almost to her neck, he then clenched them into fists before turning away without saying a word. She watched as he restlessly paced a few steps away from her. He was dressed in a long black robe. A monk's robe. It gave him an even more ominous air as he stomped from one end of the small classroom to the other in his agitation.

A few hours ago when she'd jumped out of the taxi the moment it was out of view of the academy grounds, she was resolute in her purpose. This was her investigation. What kind of reporter would she be if she left before it was over? Before the climax? She also admitted she was curious to see the pageantry of Mad Monk's Night. All the midshipmen running about in black robes carrying torches. The energy and excitement that would culminate in the lighting of the bonfire at midnight. How could she possibly leave before seeing it all? Besides, it was not as if she didn't know to suspect Mrs. Ludtz. The other victims hadn't been so lucky. That was probably why there had been no signs of a struggle. The poor things hadn't realized they were in danger until it was far too late. She knew better. It was not like she would blissfully follow Mrs. Ludtz into the dark forest, for fuck's sake! She was smarter than that, and besides, the sheriff had probably arrested her by now. How could she give up the opportunity to possibly interview Mrs. Ludtz in jail? No. She wouldn't. She couldn't. She simply had to stay.

Had to defy him.

Yes, a few hours ago in the waning daylight it had all seemed so clear. Michael was being over-protective, letting his Marine training kick into hyperdrive. She would be perfectly fine on campus among the midshipmen.

Then everything had gone wrong.

The voice in her chamber. The eerie sight of the faceless midshipmen as they scattered about the grounds. The feeling of isolation…of danger. She'd known then with icy certainty that Michael would be furious. Her arguments, which had felt so solid and definitive earlier, now seemed weak and petulant. After all, Michael could have had her escorted off campus for her duplicity…or worse. Instead, he had listened to her theories on the murder and decided to act immediately even though technically she had no proof of her suspicions. He believed in her. Despite her lies, her outright deception.

All he'd asked in return was that she be safe, even going so far as to promise her all the exclusive details about the arrest, in exchange for not having to worry about her being Ludtz's next target.

Fuck. She had made a mess of things.

"Michael, I—"

"No! No! You don't get to speak, Phoebe," he shouted as he abruptly turned to face her, his features tight with anger. "Goddammit! Do you have any idea what it felt like to hear you cry out? To see you running in terror?"

"I'm sorry. I—"

"Oh, babygirl. You're damn right you're about to be sorry."

CHAPTER 13

Phoebe took a frightened step backward as Michael ripped off his black robe. Underneath, he was wearing a pair of black cargo pants and a fitted black T-shirt. His muscled chest rose and fell with his harsh, angry breathing. Without thinking, she turned to run.

Snatching her by the upper arm, he pulled her against his hard length. "Bend your ass over that desk." The words were forced through his clenched teeth in that clipped, abrupt manner of his.

"Wh...what?"

"You heard me, princess. Bend over that desk."

"You can't mean to... to—"

"Tan your ass with my belt? You're damn right I do. You want to act like a petulant princess, you will get punished liked one."

Phoebe's cheeks heated. His playful spanking the night before had sent illicit tremors up and down her body. Being draped over his lap with his hand on her ass had come dangerously close to her recurring fantasy dream of him as a schoolmaster disciplining her, the errant schoolgirl. *But now... holy shit... he wanted her over the very desk in the very position which featured prominently in her dreams.*

Still, fantasy was one thing. Reality, on the other hand…

Shaking her head, she begged him, "Please, Michael. I promise. I'll leave."

"It's too late for that. Bend. Over."

Giving her a slight shove in the direction of the desk, he released her arm only to unbuckle his black leather belt.

Taking a tentative step toward the desk, she turned to offer one last plea. "Michael, I didn't mean to defy—"

"No more lies, Phoebe. You did mean to defy me. Deliberately putting yourself in danger. You're just sorry you got caught. Now if you don't fucking bend over that desk, I swear to God."

The rest of his unspoken threat was enough to motivate Phoebe to obey. Her rational mind screamed for her to stop, to run, to scream, to tell him no, but nothing about her feelings for Michael were rational.

Not the speed in which she fell under the spell of his rough charm, and his authoritative manner.

Not her reaction to his mere presence…or even the mention of his name.

This man enthralled her. There was no denying it.

And now after receiving his forgiveness for deceiving him, she had blatantly disregarded his order, the order of the commander of the academy, of her Commander.

She deserved this punishment, whether she wanted it or not.

Taking a deep breath, Phoebe laid her cheek on the cool surface of the desk.

"Pull down your pants. I want to see them around your thighs," he gruffly ordered.

With trembling hands, her fingers dug into the waistband of her simple black yoga pants. Pulling them over her ass, she shimmied them down till they were wrapped around her lower thighs.

Squeezing her eyes shut, she heard him take a step forward. Unable to suppress a jump when his warm fingers trailed over her lower back, Phoebe bit her lip to keep from crying out. His fingers caressed her back before lifting the thin elastic band of her thong up. Pulling on the bright pink material and forcing the thin strip of fabric to brush and tighten over her cunt. Phoebe moaned in response as her hips shifted.

He pulled harder.

Phoebe's lips fell open on a gasp. The pressure on her sensitive clit increased.

She wasn't sure if she was relieved or upset when the flimsy elastic band snapped. The thong fell to the floor.

The first snap of his belt came without warning.

She heard the crack of the leather before she truly felt it. After a moment's delay, her skin erupted in burning stings.

"Ow!" she cried out as she stood up in indignation, grasping her injured bottom.

"Back down on the desk," he growled.

Pouting, she resumed the position. Stretching her

arms out, she gripped the edge of the desk, bracing for the next strike.

The leather strap cut straight across the middle of her ass. Her skin was on fire. All her senses alert and humming. It was as if the pain were awakening her whole body.

"You *will* learn to obey my command."

His emphatic order was followed by another stinging strike from his belt. Phoebe raised up on her toes as she cried out. The belt struck her again. Her whole bottom was tormented with agonizing pricks and stings. Still, the force of his voice chastising her like the stern schoolmaster of her fantasy, the feel of the leather against her skin, the heat rising between her thighs…her hips shifted again. This time it was to grind against the sharp edge of the desk, pushing the rim against her clit, easing the building pressure.

Without thought, she moaned, "Yes, punish me."

She could hear him utter a curse below his breath, then the sound of the metal belt buckle striking the wooden floor. Next there was the scratch of the fabric of his pants as his hips rubbed against her now red and swollen skin. Phoebe bit her lip as pulsing pain mixed with anticipation. In the silence of the classroom, she could hear him lower his zipper. His large hands spanned her hips as he lifted her up onto her toes.

Leaning over her prone body, he whispered into her ear, "Oh, I'm going to punish you, princess."

She felt the rounded head of his cock moments before his thick shaft pounded into her body straight to the hilt.

Phoebe's torso wrenched up as her mouth opened on a

silent scream. The burning sting of his violent intrusion mingled with the pain from her earlier punishment. Bracing her palms against the desk, her body stayed arched as she rocked forward with the power of his thrusts.

"Oh God, it hurts!" she called out in a broken gasp.

"Good," he growled as he thrust harder, impaling her on his cock. Forcing her to take every thick inch.

Her body strained to accept him. Phoebe shifted her feet to open her legs wider, easing his entry. The swift movement of his hips caused a delicious friction deep inside her body. God help her, she loved the pain of his hard fucking.

His hand ran up her back to fist into her hair. Pulling roughly, he yanked her head back even further. She was bound and restrained within his grasp. His tongue flicked the sensitive spot below her ear before tracing a path to her shoulder. Phoebe groaned as his sharp teeth sunk into her shoulder. Marking her.

Panting from his powerful exertions, he said, "Don't ever disobey me again, baby. I couldn't stand it if I lost you."

Phoebe closed her eyes against the gathering tears. There was no mistaking the deep emotion in his voice. This large powerful Marine truly cared for her. As impossible and improbable as it sounded, given her deception.

Reaching her arm back, she grasped his neck, pulling him closer. "I won't. I promise. Never again…Commander."

Her words only spurred him on. Using his grip on her hair, he forced her body back down onto the now-warmed surface of the desk before driving into her harder and faster than before.

Her climax was so intense it was almost painful. She was only dimly aware of his own roar of completion before his large strong body fell forward on her own.

She loved the feel of his weight. Shielding her. Protecting her.

Owning her.

* * *

"You can't be serious?"

"Does it look like I'm kidding?"

After her punishment fuck in the classroom, Michael had wrapped her in his black monk robe and carried her across campus to his home. Their movements were shielded by the dark and the chaos of the midshipmen already running about the forest. He had now placed her on the bed and was standing over her with two nylon ties.

"I promised I wouldn't disobey you! I'll stay right here," she pouted.

"Forgive me if I wait for less dangerous circumstances to test that possibility out," he sniped back.

They were both thinking about what he had relayed to her during their trek to his home.

His earlier conversation with Mr. Ludtz had confirmed their suspicions. He did have an affair with Mary Bruen. The husband had also suspected that his now-unhinged wife had been responsible for his lover's death but was reluctant to go to the police, feeling enormous guilt over having caused her mental imbalance. He then had shown Michael what Mrs. Ludtz had scratched onto their bedroom wall. It was the symbol of the wendigo.

In her now-twisted mind, Mrs. Ludtz had banished one wendigo only to become one herself. It was hard to fathom how a completely normal person could become so unraveled in such a short period of time, but it was the only explanation for the bizarre murders which made sense.

The sheriff had served a search warrant on Mrs. Ludtz based on her husband's connection to one of the victims, but to no avail.

Mrs. Ludtz was nowhere to be found. They did, however, find the empty packaging for a black monk's robe and a half-eaten liver in the freezer.

The entire police department, which in this small town meant only three officers, was now looking for Mrs. Ludtz to arrest her for murder.

Problem was she was probably hiding somewhere among the midshipmen celebrating Mad Monk's Night, dressed in an identical black robe.

Getting ready to strike again at Phoebe.

It would be the perfect night for another murder. A celebration of a past evil. Chaos. Fire. The foreboding evening's celebration had it all.

"I have every available naval officer on campus as well as the entire police force in black robes scouring the crowd. Given her unstable mental state, we don't want to alert her to the search for fear she may do something rash. She would notice if there was a change in the midshipmen's celebrating, so they haven't been told. I thought I had seen her by your building which is the reason why I was on hand when you came tearing down the hallway, but she ran off when she saw me approach so now I need to get back out there without having to worry about you. She needs to be found."

She had already told him about the creepy nursery rhyme. As far as he could tell, Mrs. Ludtz had sung it through the thin, old glass of Phoebe's window in an effort to draw her out of the locked room. If Michael had not come along, who knew what might have happened.

Michael knelt on the bed, straddling her. Forcing one arm out sideways, he secured her wrist to the bedpost before doing the same to the other one.

"This is absolutely ridiculous of you," huffed Phoebe.

It was insane to go along with this, but now knowing that Mrs. Ludtz was not secured in a jail cell as she had assumed and that Michael was needed elsewhere, she felt guilty about her rash actions.

Still.

Michael paused. His large hand cupped her chin. "Do you promise to be a good girl?"

Phoebe nodded.

"I want to hear you say it, babygirl."

"I promise," she breathed only somewhat peevishly.

His warm chest brushed her cheek as he leaned over to release her wrists.

"I will tan your pert little hide if you disobey me again," he said with an exaggerated growl.

She wiggled her hips between his knees in response. Delighting in the sight of his hardening cock.

Taking her by the chin again, he leaned in. "This is

serious, Phoebe. Nothing but my responsibilities to those kids would drag me away from you. I can't go unless I know you will stay put."

Feeling the tension in his body and seeing the intent look in his eyes, she knew he was struggling between his duty to his men and his worry for her.

"I'm safe. I promise I'll stay right here. In fact, I'm going to run a bath while you're gone. You need to go and supervise the search. Besides, she's just one little old lady, how hard could it be to find her?"

"You're making light of this but the woman is still dangerous and I know she scared the fuck out of you earlier."

"She's got nothing on the King of Chinatown," scoffed Phoebe.

"Who?"

"Nothing. Look, I know you don't want to go, but we both know you have to and you should. The sooner you go, the sooner you're back."

"And when I get back, perhaps I'll tie you up again," he whispered against her lips before claiming her mouth in a searing kiss.

His dark words sent a shiver of awareness through her body. *Well now...that put a different...utterly delicious...spin on things!* It should come as no surprise to her that her domineering Marine would be into a little BDSM.... What was surprising was how much she was enjoying it. There was no denying he liked to manhandle her. Force her to his will. Fuck her almost violently. Punish her.

Own her.

She had to admit she loved it all...even the belting

punishment. She loved how she felt *claimed* by him whenever he touched her, as if she were his possession to own, protect and pleasure.

It was a more intense, heady emotion than she had ever experienced with anyone else. It was no wonder she was already half in love with the man!

It wasn't a question as to whether she could see a future with him…the question was…after all this Ludtz mess was handled…could he see a future with her?

He cupped her cunt through her yoga pants, pressing the edge of his palm in.

Phoebe bit her lip, her eyes sparkling with interest and anticipation.

"I think I could get used to tying you up. I like the idea of restraining all your chaos for my own pleasure."

"Chaos!" huffed Phoebe with feigned insult.

"Beautiful, intoxicating chaos," he amended as he leaned down to kiss her forehead. "And I am loving every minute of it."

She blushed as she watched him stand up and once more don the black monk robe. Pulling the hood up, he gave her a seductive wink before heading back into the night.

Phoebe smiled. She was certain the answer was yes, that man could definitely see a future with her too!

* * *

STILL FEELING a tingling between her thighs, Phoebe rose and headed into the bathroom, intent on behaving herself and running a bath like she'd told Michael she would.

He'd only been gone a few minutes when she heard the sound of his returning footsteps.

"Ha! I knew it! I knew this was a test to see if I would obey without a fuss! I knew you'd come right back," called out Phoebe triumphantly from the bathroom as she turned to walk back into the bedroom, pleased she had proven to Michael her sole purpose wasn't to make his life difficult by defying him at every turn.

A black-hooded figure appeared in the doorway.

It wasn't Michael.

* * *

Hush now, Phoebe, do not you fear
Never mind, Phoebe, the Mad Monk is near

Mrs. Ludtz began to sing in that sickly child-like voice as she approached Phoebe holding a gun and several zip ties.

Phoebe screamed for help as she realized she was trapped inside the bathroom.

Still Mrs. Ludtz sang.

Never mind, Phoebe, the Mad Monk is near

Lashing out, Mrs. Ludtz grabbed one of her arms with surprising strength, wrenching her forward and jabbing a needle into Phoebe's neck in one smooth practiced motion.

Phoebe's last conscious thought was of Michael...and how pissed he was going to be when he returned to find her gone.

CHAPTER 14

She could feel her body being jostled and dragged but was powerless to fight back. It was as if she were moving through sand. Everything seemed slow and muted. Phoebe felt a blast of cold air against her cheek. Mrs. Ludtz must have taken her outside. Once again she felt as if she were being dragged, then some kind of chilled metal surface brushed her bare arm. Phoebe shivered. Her thin yoga pants and T-shirt were no match for the October wind whipping off the bay. There was a hand on her head, forcing her down, pushing her body into a bent position. Although she couldn't open her eyes, she could feel a heavy musty canvas draping being tossed over her. Then everything seemed to move again. Phoebe could hear the crunch of gravel and the distant excited shouts of the midshipmen. Swallowing down a wave of nausea, Phoebe tried to force her lips to move, to scream for help. All that came out was a weak groan as she was thrown about in what must have been a wheelbarrow.

"Hello there. Captain Dobson was looking for you," said Mrs. Ludtz.

Phoebe struggled to maintain consciousness. Struggled to make out the conversation Mrs. Ludtz seemed to be having with a midshipman but whatever Mrs. Ludtz had stuck in her neck was taking full effect.

"Are you sure, Mrs. Ludtz? I'm supposed to be guarding the bonfire."

"He seemed pretty insistent. I'll stay here and keep watch till you return. I brought a wheelbarrow full of sand to top off all the buckets. You can help me when you return."

"Thanks, Mrs. Ludtz. I'll be right back."

No! Don't leave me with her! Phoebe's mind raged and fought but the drug was too strong.

All sound became muted. She could no longer feel her body.

Everything went black.

* * *

The cold hard feel of the...something.

The smell of wood and...something else...something acrid and strong.

The raucous shouts and...and what?

Bright hazy spots of color.

Slowly Phoebe came awake. Desperately, she tried to hold on to whatever she could sense, any sort of anchor to bring her back to consciousness.

The cold hard feel of the ground.

The smell of pine needles and...what?

The raucous shouts and chanting.
Bright spots of orange and red.

Languidly, everything was becoming clearer. Nothing was distinct though; it was as if she were experiencing it all underwater. Lying on her side, she tried to move her arms, to push herself up to a sitting position but it was no use. Her arms were secured behind her back. Willing her limbs to move, she tested her legs. They too were tied. Gradually her senses were awakening, coming out of their drugged fog.

She was lying in the grass.
There was the smell of wood and... gasoline.
Male voices were chanting... Burn the Mad Monk! Burn the Mad Monk!
Flames. Fire. Dancing fire surrounding her.

A primal surge of survival instinct ripped through her body. Using her core, Phoebe forced her body into a sitting position. She was in an enclosed space. Large black poles formed a sort of teepee around her. There was no exit. Just one continuous circle of poles. Through the cracks in the poles she could see indistinct forms and torches.

Oh my fucking God! She was inside the bonfire!

A shower of sparks rained down on her bare feet as wisps of smoke began to curl and move between the wooden poles. Panicked, Phoebe shifted backward. They must have lit the bonfire. Finally finding her voice, she began to scream with every ounce of strength she possessed.

Burn the Mad Monk! Burn the Mad Monk!

As the flames began to spread from pole to pole, the chanting became louder. No one could hear her screams. Phoebe tried to kick at the wooden poles but it was no use. She knew from having watched the men build the wooden teepee that would become the bonfire that they had secured each pole with heavy wire to prevent the structure from collapsing. Why! Why hadn't it occurred to Michael or her that Mrs. Ludtz would be attracted to the bonfire? It was perfect. It would allow her to succeed where she had failed with the first two victims.

It would allow her to burn her victim alive…to burn Phoebe alive…to fulfill the lore of the wendigo.

The confined space was now brightly lit as the flames traveled from pole to pole. She choked as thick smoke began to surround her. She gave out one last feeble scream before collapsing backward.

Her thoughts were of Michael and what could have been.

"Michael," she cried out with her last breath.

* * *

"Did you hear something?" asked Michael as he watched the flames from the fire begin to creep up the poles, lighting the night sky.

"Can't hear nothing over all this shouting," groused the sheriff. "As I said, there's no trace of her. She's crazy but not so crazy as to have eluded all detection until now. Maybe the robe was to throw us off the scent. She could be halfway to California for all we know."

Michael crossed his arms over his chest as he took in what the sheriff was trying to tell him. "No,' he disagreed. "I think the only reason why she eluded detection is that no one thought to really look into the matter until Phoebe came along, otherwise we would have easily learned of the connection between Mrs. Ludtz and the first victim. I think the woman is no longer stable or thinking clearly. She's here all right."

They had searched the woods and surrounding area. There was no trace of her.

Once again, Michael was relieved to know Phoebe was safe and sound in his home…in his bathtub or perhaps his bed. He smiled at the thought of how her green eyes sparkled as her pretty cheeks tinged with pink when she'd been caught disobeying. Damn she was fun when she was mad! When this was all over, he was going to ask her to stay. He wasn't sure how life with him at the academy could compete with all New York had to offer, but he was damn well going to try. In the short time he had known her he now couldn't imagine life without her. She was so full of energy and fire. Challenging him at every turn. He loved how she stood up to him. Never intimidated by his rank or even his size.

After learning her true name, he had devoured every article she had ever written, admiring her all the more for her intelligence and commitment to a story. Although those articles also had had him clenching his fists in frustration and fear. It was obvious this was not the first time she had run headlong into danger for the sake of a story. The one about the mafia and the sanitation scandal came to mind as did the one about the sex trafficking ring. It was only a matter of time before she got herself in too deep. Well, as far as he was concerned, she had him to protect her now. Whether it was in New York or at the academy, he planned to be by her side. He just hoped she felt the same way.

Lost in his thoughts, he watched as the dark outline of the teepee made from wooden poles was engulfed in flames. Soon it would reach the stuffed dummy meant to be the Mad Monk effigy.

Again, he thought he heard a scream.

"You don't hear that?" he asked the sheriff again.

A midshipman standing nearby responded, "Isn't it great, Commander? We put a small speaker in the dummy so that it would sound like the Mad Monk was screaming!"

The sheriff shook his head. "Sounds damn creepy to me, but then I never understood this whole Mad Monk Night business anyhow."

Michael was only partially listening…there was just something about that scream….

"Goddammit! Everyone stop. Silence!" roared Michael.

Every midshipman immediately stilled at his command.

There it was again but fainter…Phoebe.

"It's not the speaker. Phoebe is trapped inside the bonfire," shouted Michael as he lunged toward the burning wooden structure.

Strong hands pulled him back. Michael fought against the restraint.

"Commander! Stop! You can't just pull on the poles,

the whole thing could collapse on her," advised Mark Dobson.

Michael stopped struggling. Jesus Christ! Phoebe! He needed to think, to strategize. Taking in the scene, he calmed his mind and focused. Surrounding the bonfire were buckets of sand and numerous fire extinguishers for safety. He also reasoned that it had to have been Mrs. Ludtz who had put Phoebe there, which meant the woman had to have found an open space in the poles to push Phoebe through. If he could find that space, he could drag her out to safety. Praying to God she was still alive.

"You're right, Captain. Organize the men. Grab the buckets and extinguishers and get the flames out. Sheriff, go left. I'll go right. Search through the flames for any gaps in the poles," shouted Michael.

Michael began to circle the large structure, searching for a gap. Desperately listening for Phoebe's cries. If she was still screaming it meant she was still alive and there was still hope. He could hear the shouts of alarm roll through the midshipmen like a wave. Everyone sprang into action.

He met up with the sheriff on the other side. "Anything?"

"No. We need these flames out," responded the sheriff, his jaw tight with anxiety.

"My men are working on it. Keep looking."

Michael kept up his search. Fear gnawed at his gut. The only frantic thought in his mind played over and over again.

I can't lose her.
I can't lose her.

I can't lose her.

Finally, he saw his opening. A midshipman had tossed a bucket of sand at the base of the bonfire. Michael could see a small gap. He would barely be able to get his arm and shoulder in but it would have to be enough. With Phoebe's petite frame, he was certain that was how she'd been forced inside the structure. Falling to his knees, he shouted for help as he braced his hands against the still-smoldering poles. Ignoring the intense, searing pain from the heat, he pushed his arm through and swung it in an arc, searching for her.

Nothing.

He swung his arm around in an arc again.

Nothing.

She was in there. He was certain of it.

Shoving his shoulders against the two poles, he looked up to see the now-compromised structure as it shifted and groaned.

"Get back! Get back!" he shouted to his men.

"But Professor Phoebe, Commander! We're not leaving her to die!" exclaimed one of the midshipmen from her class as the others nodded resolutely.

Michael swung his arm again. This time he felt it. The soft fabric of her pants. Running his hand down her calf, he latched onto her ankle as if both their lives depended on it.

Because they did.

There was no life for him without her…of that he was now certain.

"Ready men? Pull on my legs!" shouted Michael.

He could feel strong hands grab his legs and yank

hard. When his right arm cleared the structure with Phoebe's slim leg, he reached his left arm in to grab her other ankle.

"Pull," he shouted.

"Heave," yelled Captain Dobson to the men.

Michael's body slid along the now-muddied ground. The sound of splintering wood rent the air. The structure swayed.

"Heave, men! Heave!"

Another pull and both Michael and Phoebe were free of the structure but not out of danger. Rising to his feet, he swept her inert form into his arms and ran, shouting for his men to follow.

They had barely cleared the space before there was the ghastly sound of wood splintering and cracking. One by one the poles began to fall like dominoes, till there was nothing but a still-smoking heap of logs.

Michael fell to his knees with Phoebe still clasped in his arms. Breathing heavily, he could only hold her.

Never in his life had he been more afraid.

She was so still.

He didn't want to look down into her face. Didn't want to confirm what he feared…that he had been too late. That he had failed to protect his love.

"Commander," said a gentle yet anxious voice.

Michael looked up into the determined eyes of one of his midshipmen. He had a first aid kit at his feet.

"Commander, you have to put her down. We have to check for signs of life."

His men had taken off their robes to create a makeshift bed for Phoebe so she wouldn't be on the cold ground.

Michael laid her down gently. Black smudges of soot marred her nose and mouth; the rest of her face was deathly pale. Pinching her nose between two fingers, he pressed his lips to her own and breathed into her. He could hear the distant sirens from the ambulance as it drove up onto the grassy quad.

He breathed into her again.

And again.

Nothing.

"Goddammit, princess. You better not fucking die on me. I command you to open your eyes," he shouted in frustration.

Her eyelids fluttered then opened. Her beautiful green eyes, shimmering with tears.

"I don't think you're allowed to talk to me like that," she whispered. Her voice hoarse and raw from the smoke inhalation.

Michael's own eyes teared up. Cupping her face with his hand, he replied, "Finally, a command you obeyed!"

The rest of their conversation was drowned out by exuberant shouts of "Hooyah!"

* * *

THE PARAMEDICS PLACED an oxygen mask over her face and strapped her to the gurney. All the while, his men looked on anxiously. It seemed he was not the only one Phoebe had charmed in her short time at the academy.

Looking over his shoulder, Michael saw the sheriff standing nearby. "You had better hope you find that woman before I do, Sheriff," he warned.

The sheriff nodded. "Wouldn't blame you one bit, Colonel. You head on to the hospital. We'll find her. Don't you worry about that."

Michael gave the older man a nod before hopping into the ambulance beside Phoebe.

CHAPTER 15

Two weeks later

"After stealing a fisherman's boat and leading the local police in a chase across Buzzards Bay, the suspect Anne Ludtz was finally apprehended with the help of several midshipmen and their commander, Lieutenant Colonel Michael Lawson, who also gave chase in the Puller Academy boats. She is currently under psychiatric care as she awaits a trial date on two counts of first-degree murder and one count of attempted murder," read Henry aloud. Picking up his cigar, he took a long drag before turning to Phoebe. "Helluva job, Wilson. Helluva job!"

Phoebe plucked the cigar from his fingers and snubbed it out in the ashtray on his desk.

"Hey, it's after noon! I'm allowed," complained Henry.

"Let's just say I have a whole new appreciation for life and you should too," responded Phoebe as she took a sip of her usual mocha latte, wrinkling her nose at the harsh, burnt coffee taste. It wasn't as good as the mocha lattes from the little cafe Amber and she frequented in Buzzards Bay.

Buzzards Bay.

She actually missed the place. Missed the raw beauty of the bay at sunrise. Missed the challenge of lighting a spark in her midshipmen students about Dickens or Shakespeare. Missed the camaraderie of the other teachers.

She especially missed Michael.

For days after the bonfire, he'd never left her side. He'd even insisted on sleeping on a cot in her hospital room rather than going home to rest.

If she hadn't been certain before, her time spent together with him then with his constant caring attention sealed her fate. She was head over heels in love with the man.

It was a strangely wonderful time. Sure, she'd had to suffer through chest scans and blood tests and the whole gamut to make sure there wasn't any real damage from her brush with death but through it all…there was Michael. He entertained her by reading poetry. She especially loved when he read from Lord Byron. His dark, deep voice was a perfect match for the moody, mercurial poet's poems. They talked for hours about their childhoods, his time in the military and all sorts of the silly things people talk about to get to know one another.

They talked about everything, except the future.

It seemed like neither wanted to broach the subject. Whether it was because they were afraid of what the other may say or even more afraid of what they might not…talk of love and a future together remained unspoken. Soon it came time for her to leave, to return to her old life in New York.

Secretly, she kept hoping he would command her to stay, but he hadn't.

He just let her go.

Since then, there had been long phone conversations and emails, mostly about the case against Ludtz. No mention of her returning to the academy or of love.

And worse, she had sent him the article on Ludtz earlier this morning and hadn't heard a word from him. She had to be fair in her reporting. Phoebe had hoped he would understand that. It wasn't her fault the Navy had looked the other way for so long. She did her best to be impartial and not lambaste them like other reporters would have done, but the truth was the truth. Besides, the Navy made good in the end. If it hadn't been for Michael's help, Ludtz may never have been found out and caught.

"Are you even listening to me?" groused Henry.

"Sorry, what?"

"I asked what you plan to do next. What have you got for me?"

"There's talk of a bribery scandal about to break in the mayor's office," responded Phoebe absentmindedly.

Henry nodded. "Could have some legs on it. What else?"

"Um… there's that thing about the tainted rice in China. A source tells me some of it might have made its way into US products."

"That thing that killed all the kids?"

Phoebe nodded her head.

"That sounds promising. Nothing like a good scare to sell newspapers."

"Uh huh."

"Wilson. Are you even paying attention? Ever since you got back from that Buzzard assignment it's like your heart isn't in it anymore."

She could never get anything past Henry. "You're not going to like this but I don't think it is."

Henry nodded sagely. "Is it that commander fella, the one you wrote about?"

"Why would you say that?" Phoebe shifted in her seat as her cheeks began to heat.

Henry held up the newspaper, giving it a tap with his index finger. "Because you make the guy sound like Batman and Superman all rolled into one."

Her cheeks grew even hotter. "You've been hanging around Jimmy and his stupid comic books too much."

Pointing at her with one stubby finger, Henry rejoined, "And you're ignoring the facts."

Phoebe toyed with the cardboard sleeve of her empty mocha latte cup. "I don't know what you mean."

"You love him, Phoebe. It's as plain as the nose on your face."

She looked up and met Henry's sympathetic eyes. "Yeah, but what does that get me? I have a career. Women from my generation aren't supposed to give that shit up for love."

Henry shrugged. "There's nothing that says you can't freelance once in a while and besides…to my way of thinking…it's more what you're gaining then giving up."

"You're my boss. Aren't you supposed to be convincing me to stay?"

He nodded. "I'm your boss…but I'm also practically a father to you. And I say to hell with this dog and pony show. Go get your soldier!"

"Marine," said Phoebe without thinking.

"Is there a difference?"

Phoebe jumped up and gave Henry a hug around the neck. "I've been told many times there is." Laughing as she grabbed her shoulder bag and prepared to leave, Phoebe was already checking her phone for flights out of New York when there was a huge commotion outside Henry's office.

She opened the door to see Michael marching through the *Ledger* offices in full dress uniform.

He looked magnificent, over six feet of impressive uniform, muscle and…anger? Uh oh…he also looked pissed as hell, thought Phoebe as she took in his lowered brow and clenched jaw.

Phoebe defiantly placed her hands on her hips. Narrowing her eyes, she prepared to meet him head on. "Nothing I wrote in that article was untrue, so if you've got a problem with it, then you are not the man I thought you were!"

Without missing a step or saying a word, Michael swooped down and lifted Phoebe into his arms. He turned and started to walk out of the office.

"What are you doing?" exclaimed Phoebe as she was forced to grab onto his neck.

"I don't give a damn about that article. I tried to be a gentleman. Tried to give you space to make the right decision, but my patience is at an end, babygirl. You're mine and I'm taking you home," ground out Michael as his determined gaze pierced her astonished one.

"Do I get a say in this?"

"No."

God, she loved this arrogant, demanding man!

"Well, are you going to at least admit that you love me?" huffed Phoebe as her cheeks heated knowing they were being observed by every member of the *Ledger's* staff.

Giving her a suggestive look, he said, "I'm going to do a lot more than just admit I love you, princess. I'm going to make you scream who's your Commander."

Burying her head in his neck, Phoebe tried to hide her satisfied smile. "You're being very *An Officer and A Gentleman* right now," she teased.

Michael's lips quirked. "Gere's character was a naval officer candidate. I'm a Marine officer."

Flicking the tip of her tongue against the edge of her teeth, Phoebe grinned. She loved baiting him. "What's the difference?"

His arms gripped her tighter. "I plan to spend a lifetime showing you."

EPILOGUE

Two years later

"Time to wake up, Professor Lawson."

Phoebe opened her eyes and smiled at Michael.

"Or should I say Dr. Lawson?" he asked with a wink. "You don't want to miss your first class of the fall semester."

Phoebe had taken the last two years to earn her doctorate in English Literature so she could become a full professor at Puller Academy. Not a day had gone by where she regretted leaving her life in New York behind to be with Michael. The murder case which brought them together was a distant memory but their life hadn't become any less exciting. With Michael at the helm as commander, Puller Academy had finally made the transition into a co-ed military academy. The addition of women had added a whole new energy and dynamic to the school, and kept them both busy creating all new procedures, classes and traditions.

She still liked to challenge and fight with Michael, keeping him on his toes…or as he would call it…pushing his buttons, but oh it was so much fun to make up with him! Her now-husband had a penchant for taking her in semi-private places around campus, like the library, gymnasium and empty classrooms. It was a miracle they hadn't got gotten caught yet…although they did have several close calls which made it that much more exciting for them both.

He had also gotten quite creative with his punishments.

Pulling on her bound right wrist which was secured to the bedpost with a black silk tie, she teased, "Then perhaps you had better untie me."

Michael leaned in to give her a quick kiss before untying her wrist. As she got out of bed, he swatted her ass with a rolled up newspaper.

"Hey!" Phoebe laughed as she scooted out of the way.

"Thought you might like to see your latest article. Henry sent up a copy."

To Henry's delight, she had continued to write the occasional feature piece for the *Ledger*, usually during the summer or winter breaks. Michael wrapped his arms around her waist from behind as she opened the newspaper to check out her headline and article.

Pushing her long soft curls aside, Michael kissed her on the neck just below her ear. "So, have you decided what your next project will be?"

"What do you mean?"

"The school is co-ed and you have your doctorate which means you now have free time on your hands, which I know from experience can be very dangerous. I need to keep you occupied and by my side so you don't go running off halfway across the country to chase down some crazy headline for the *Ledger*."

Turning in his arms, Phoebe wrapped her arms around his neck. "There was a headline I was particularly interested in, but I think it's something only the school newspaper would print."

His brow lowered. "What would that be?"

"Lieutenant Colonel Michael Lawson and Dr. Phoebe Lawson welcome first child."

"Are you pregnant?" asked an astonished Michael as he gripped her hips and lifted her into the air.

"Why, Commander! I don't think you're allowed to ask an employee that," teased Phoebe with false affront.

"I'm asking anyway," he growled as he carried her back to the bed. Laying her down among the rumpled covers, he covered her body with his own.

Running her fingernails down his naked, muscled chest, she cooed, "Maybe if you ask me nicely, I'll tell you."

"Oh, baby, I'm a Marine. We don't do…nice." Michael ran his hand over her stomach to cup one full breast as he nipped at her shoulder.

"I wouldn't have it any other way," said Phoebe.

* * *

Later that night, Michael surprised her with a celebratory dinner. He made them spaghetti and meatballs, her favorite. He drank wine. She had grape juice.

The end.

ABOUT ZOE BLAKE

Zoe Blake is the USA Today Bestselling Author of the romantic suspense sagas The Diamanti Billionaire Dynasty & The Cavalieri Billionaire Legacy inspired by her own heritage as well as her obsession with jewelry, travel, and the salacious gossip of history's most infamous families.

She delights in writing Dark Romance books filled with overly possessive billionaires, taboo scenes, and unexpected twists. She usually spends her ill-gotten gains on martinis, travels, and red lipstick. Since she can barely boil water, she's lucky enough to be married to a sexy Chef.

ALSO BY ZOE BLAKE

THE SURRENDER SERIES

An Enemies to Lovers Romance

Ruthless Surrender

I know her darkest secret and am just ruthless enough to use it against her.

Whether she likes it or not, I'm the only one who can help her, but I do nothing for free.

My price is her complete surrender.

She can hate me all she wants, as long as she pays with her body.

And if she tries to run?

That will just cost her more.

Rebellious Surrender

First, she tried to kill me.

Then she ran.

Hunting her down will be my pleasure and her pain.

Nobody defies me and gets away with it, especially not her.

My pretty captive is about to learn her rebelliousness has consequences.

I'll settle for nothing less than her complete surrender.

Reckless Surrender

Her first mistake was lying to me.

Did she actually think I would let her get away with this deception?

I was going to make her pay for every lie that slipped from those gorgeous lips.

She may think this is just a game of teacher and naughty schoolgirl, but I have a surprise for her.

I only play games I can win, and my prize will be her complete surrender.

Relentless Surrender

She's mine… she just doesn't know it yet.

Stubborn and feisty as hell, she's going to fight me every step of the way.

What she doesn't understand is, I'm a Marine… and we never back down.

If we see a target we want… we take it.

It's as simple as that.

And I want her.

Badly.

RUTHLESS OBSESSION SERIES

A Dark Mafia Romance

Sweet Cruelty

Dimitri & Emma's story

It was an innocent mistake.

She knocked on the wrong door.

Mine.

If I were a better man, I would've just let her go.

But I'm not.

I'm a cruel bastard.

I ruthlessly claimed her virtue for my own.

It should have been enough.

But it wasn't.

I needed more.

Craved it.

She became my obsession.

Her sweetness and purity taunted my dark soul.

The need to possess her nearly drove me mad.

A Russian arms dealer had no business pursuing a naive librarian student.

She didn't belong in my world.

I would bring her only pain.

But it was too late…

She was mine and I was keeping her.

Sweet Depravity

Vaska & Mary's story

The moment she opened those gorgeous red lips to tell me no, she was mine.

I was a powerful Russian arms dealer and she was an innocent schoolteacher.

If she had a choice, she'd run as far away from me as possible.

Unfortunately for her, I wasn't giving her one.

I wasn't just going to take her; I was going to take over her entire world.

Where she lived.

What she ate.

Where she worked.

All would be under my control.

Call it obsession.

Call it depravity.

I don't give a damn… as long as you call her mine.

Sweet Savagery

Ivan & Dylan's Story

I was a savage bent on claiming her as punishment for her family's mistakes.

As a powerful Russian Arms dealer, no one steals from me and gets away with it.

She was an innocent pawn in a dangerous game.

She had no idea the package her uncle sent her from Russia contained my stolen money.

If I were a good man, I would let her return the money and leave.

If I were a gentleman, I might even let her keep some of it just for frightening her.

As I stared down at the beautiful living doll stretched out before me like a virgin sacrifice,

I thanked God for every sin and misdeed that had blackened my cold heart.

I was not a good man.

I sure as hell wasn't a gentleman… and I had no intention of letting her go.

She was mine now.

And no one takes what's mine.

Sweet Brutality

Maxim & Carinna's story

The more she fights me, the more I want her.

It's that beautiful, sassy mouth of hers.

It makes me want to push her to her knees and dominate her, like the brutal savage I am.

As a Russian Arms dealer, I should not be ruthlessly pursuing an innocent college student like her, but that would not stop me.

A twist of fate may have brought us together, but it is my twisted obsession that will hold her captive as my own treasured possession.

She is mine now.

I dare you to try and take her from me.

Sweet Ferocity

Luka & Katie's Story

I was a mafia mercenary only hired to find her, but now I'm going to keep her.

She is a Russian mafia princess, kidnapped to be used as a pawn in a dangerous territory war.

Saving her was my job. Keeping her safe had become my obsession.

Every move she makes, I am in the shadows, watching.

I was like a feral animal: cruel, violent, and selfishly out for my own needs. Until her.

Now, I will make her mine by any means necessary.

I am her protector, but no one is going to protect her from me.

IVANOV CRIME FAMILY TRILOGY

A Dark Mafia Romance

Savage Vow

Gregor & Samara's story

I took her innocence as payment.

She was far too young and naïve to be betrothed to a monster like me.

I would bring only pain and darkness into her sheltered world.

That's why she ran.

I should've just let her go…

She never asked to marry into a powerful Russian mafia family.

None of this was her choice.

Unfortunately for her, I don't care.

I own her… and after three years of searching… I've found her.

My runaway bride was about to learn disobedience has consequences… punishing ones.

Having her in my arms and under my control had become an obsession.

Nothing was going to keep me from claiming her before the eyes of God and man.

She's finally mine… and I'm never letting her go.

Vicious Oath

Damien & Yelena's story

When I give an order, I expect it to be obeyed.

She's too smart for her own good, and it's going to get her killed.

Against my better judgement, I put her under the protection of my powerful Russian mafia family.

So imagine my anger when the little minx ran.

For three long years I've been on her trail, always one step behind.

Finding and claiming her had become an obsession.

It was getting harder to rein in my driving need to possess her… to own her.

But now the chase is over.

I've found her.

Soon she will be mine.

And I plan to make it official, even if I have to drag her kicking and screaming to the altar.

This time… there will be no escape from me.

Betrayed Honor

Mikhail & Nadia's story

Her innocence was going to get her killed.

That was if I didn't get to her first.

She's the protected little sister of the powerful Ivanov Russian mafia family - the very definition of forbidden.

It's always been my job, as their Head of Security, to watch over her but never to touch.

That ends today.

She disobeyed me and put herself in danger.

It was time to take her in hand.

I'm the only one who can save her and I will fight anyone who tries to stop me, including her brothers.

Honor and loyalty be damned.

She's mine now.

For a list of All of Zoe Blake's Books Visit her Website!

www.zblakebooks.com

Printed in Great Britain
by Amazon